I0458219

DUGHALL

Travis McGuire

ISBN 978-0-9898897-2-8

Published by The People's Ink

www.peoples-ink.com

In memory of Justin Turner

DUGHALL

One

Dmitri looked over from his Trans Am and grinned. I nodded and turned toward the moonlit blacktop road where our headlights blazed over the crooked bumps and yellow lines. Vicky stood in the middle of the road, a yellow handkerchief in her hand. I looked at the cornfields to my left, their green stalks and leaves playing catch with the wind. To the right were a hundred elm, maple and oak, canopy crowned with all the stars of the night. Spread before me was my Nova's gray hood, glowing a luminescent blue under the bright moonlight. I breathed in the sweet aroma of corn and summer river bottom air.

You boys ready? Vicky shouted over the rumble of exhaust pounding the pavement.

We revved our engines. She raised the handkerchief and quickly brought it down to her waist. As it fell, my foot pressed the pedal. The car twisted and tugged. The rear tires grabbed. I could see the Trans Am's headlights next to the middle of my fender. I gave the Nova more gas until the pedal touched the floor. The engine growled as the RPMs went over 6,000. I slapped the shifter forward, ratcheting into the next gear, lunging ahead and away from the Trans Am. Again I shifted. The Trans Am's headlights even with my door as we crossed the jagged orange line. I let off the gas. The engine emitting a loud sigh.

I was in the left lane and slowed until Dmitri passed me. He flew by, slammed on his brakes and slid past, spinning his tires and recklessly swung the back of the Trans Am sideways in the road. Tires belched smoke. He straightened and gunned it back to the starting line. I slowed the Nova, preparing to follow when something caught my eye. A woman. She darted into the middle of the highway and somehow I thought it was Vicky coming to congratulate me. She walked into the road waving.

Though the Nova was still moving forward at around sixty miles an hour, it seemed to be puttering at two. Nearing her, I saw it wasn't Vicky. Perhaps she needed a lift. Maybe her car broke down. I pushed the brakes and realized I was going much too fast to stop without hitting her unless she moved. I swerved to the left but the car's tires were not meant for rapid turns. It fishtailed and as I struggled to correct, she moved again.

She was now directly in front of my driver's headlight. Her pink shirt looked brighter now. All its intricacies visible. Wrinkles. Folds. The outline of her breasts. Her flesh shone. Tanned soft. I pushed so hard on the pedal that I thought it would go through the floorboard. I smelled hot brakes and tires.

I could not stop. Her face contorted as she anticipated the impact. But her eyes were curious, almost calm. I stared into them as the Nova connected with her. She braced herself. Perhaps it was her life meandering through her third eye. Perhaps she wished she were Superwoman. Able to smash the car with her fist. Whatever those thoughts, her eyes seemed peaceful now. I saw her belly curve backward in the impact. Her hands outstretched toward me as if I were her savior.

I shut my eyes. Glass crackled. Tires squealed. The car slid to a stop. I opened my eyes, the headlights pointed off the road into the dense trees and brush. The car rumbled and shook. I thought I was dreaming until I looked up and saw the windshield. Cracked. Caved in. Bloody. I was afraid to look to my left but I did. She lay motionless. Jeans half off. Butt exposed. Arms and legs akimbo. I did not see her breathing.

Two

That night, in July of 1999, had started out like any Saturday in Baumgras, Missouri. I had been turning wrenches at the Garage when Dmitri called. He wanted to get his Trans Am ready to race that night. Dmitri was nineteen, the same age as me and was a handsome lean muscled cigarette puffing fool, a modern James Dean, who even in my youth I knew would die young. He worked as a mobile mechanic and first responder filling his time between with booze, drugs and motorsports.

I walked out of work to my 1970 Chevrolet Nova. Gritty gray primer. A dentless, rust-free beauty with five spoke star wheels wrapped in smooth rubber. She sat, always ready. Her headlights round, the grill's horizontal chrome twinkling, front bumper leaning toward concrete, her rear slanted up, wide tires filling the wheel well. Interior was meticulous, no frills. Gauges all stock but for the large tachometer rising from behind the steering wheel. There was no carpet and black race seats sat on the raw, painted floorboards. Between the seats, a hammerhead knobbed chrome ratchet shifter rose, mechanical, phallic. A rollcage curved behind the seats and rose nearly to the headliner. Black original backseat remained intact. I turned the key. She belched. Engine a fast drumbeat. Under the hammerhead knob on the shifter was a trigger to shift from park to reverse to neutral and to D, 2, 1. I pulled up on the trigger and back on the shifter into D. Engine dropping tempo, I took off toward Dmitri's.

I pulled into his driveway. Rusty wrecked cars rested, weeds growing through haphazard unrecognizable rotting metal. A ring of trees surrounded it all. In the middle of the lot sat his trailer, truck and Trans Am. Had Dmitri applied himself he would have been a much better mechanic than myself, but he drank too much and was out for only the extremes in life. I didn't mind helping him with his car though. Dmitri stood by his truck, beer and cigarette in hand.

Dughall, you fucker! Glad to see ya!

Likewise. You gonna give me a beer or what?

He laughed, tossing me one from the cooler nearby. We spent the afternoon tuning the cars and he telling stories.

Gaddam Dughall, ya shoulda been there! Bobby had that massive Caddy engine in the truck, had more torque than an Army tank. Bobby floored that muther, shifting through all four gears on tha highway. That cop just tryin to catch us but Bobby just kept'er to tha floor, roasting that clutch and boy that engine was wound tight! Tighter than I ever heard'er. We were laughing all the way. That cop couldn't catch us but then outta nowhere came that damn Patrol Mustang loaded with nitrous and a supercharger maybe even a turbo. It came whining up behind us lights flashing in the mirrors. Then Bobby, crazy fucker just turned offa the road into the ditch, probably the only time I ever been scared in an automobile and that's sayin somethin. We bumped and jumped cross that highway onto a gravel road and we knew all those gravel roads ya know an lost those fuckers. Crazy shit!

The more the afternoon progressed the more excited Dmitri became. Ready to race. Drink. Hook up with some girl. At six o'clock we headed to town to grab a bite at Spaghetti's, an inexpensive Italian restaurant. I got spaghetti and fruit punch. We finished and pulled out of the parking lot with subsequent burnouts. Dmitri first.

Dmitri's Trans Am was a bit slower than my Nova but did a nasty burnout. I could hardly see as I followed his sideways burnout with one of my own, leaving the Boulevard filled with smoke, the smell of burning rubber and racing fuel. We lunged to each stop light and turned into Burger Stand's parking lot.

Frank Clinton was already waiting for us. He smoked a cigarette. Frank was a quiet guy, a computer science major who was always smoking. He drove a gorgeous stock 1971 Dodge Charger he had restored himself. We talked for a while about the events of last weekend when I had accidentally broken the back window out of Johnny Bartholomew's truck with a piece of wood. I didn't think that it would bounce back up out of the bed and into the window. We talked about races and cars and girls until a few cute ones in a silver Mustang drove by with the passenger hanging out of the window. It was time to drive. The guys nodded when I told them I was going to cruise. They decided to wait for others to show.

I hopped in the Nova and turned the key forward. The V-8 gurgled, grumbled and with a roar shook the car. I pushed the pedal halfway to the floor once. The exhaust pipe pressure thumped against the pavement. The car briefly lurched as I bumped the floor shifter into reverse. It rolled back and I tapped the shifter with the palm of my hand, pushing it into drive. I put my left foot on the brake and my right on the gas. Engine revved. Tires spun.

In the rear view mirror, tire smoke floated over their heads. I pulled out into the street and gunned it again. The steering wheel pulled one way and the rear of the car swung out the other. I smiled. The Nova straightened, tires still spinning. Sixty came quick. I let off the gas until the Nova slowed to the posted speed limit of forty. For the next hour I drove, turning around at the west end car wash and the music store on the east side. Every once in a while, I took the back streets where I found some solitude. When I got back to Burger Stand, more cars had arrived. It was a lot for our parking lot, even on this perfect summer evening. Vicky was the first to greet me. She screamed, her small frame leaping, onto me hugging me tight.

Dughall!

Hey Vicky, how're you?

Great! I tried to wave you down before you pulled

out while ago.

I didn't see you.

Probably because of all that tire smoke! You know it's only cool so many times.

She smiled as she said it.

Frank intervened, Hey man. Nice burnout. You see the new Chevelle cruising? He stopped by and wants to race ya. It sounds wicked.

I haven't seen him. I'm already racing Dmitri tonight. If the Nova's still runnin good maybe I'll race him.

He said he'd be back after he fueled up.

Can I ride? Vicky said.

Yeah Vicky, you can ride as long as you wear a helmet and harness.

I know your rules, she said.

I went to my car to make sure I had a helmet but something felt wrong. My hands shook. It was difficult to open the trunk. I hoped no one was watching. The trunk popped open and I took slow steady breaths trying to calm my nerves. I never got this nervous. Maybe I shouldn't race.

I shut the trunk as the Chevelle pulled into the lot. It looked good in understated white paint and chrome. The engine sounded healthy, similar to the Nova. The driver revved the engine. I was reluctant and for a moment I stood still. I told myself it was just the jitters. I went over and told Vicky I didn't have a helmet for her. We rolled out to the old highway. Cars pulsing on the asphalt through the cornfields and river bottom. That's when things changed.

Three

I sat there. I don't know how long. Yells came from behind but I could not understand them. A car rumbled behind me. Dmitri. He jumped out of the Trans Am and ran up to me.

You okay man? You hit a deer or something?

I pointed. He glanced over and in the moonlight we stared at the motionless body.

Oh fuck! he yelled as he grabbed a bag out of his car and rushed over to her.

I gathered myself, perhaps out of admiration for his quick action and yelled, Do you need me to help?

He didn't glance up but said, No, I need you to stay right there.

I lit a cigarette, opened the car door and started to rise. As I sat up I noticed my chest heavy and moving. It felt like a dentist was pulling a lead vest off me like a blanket. Broken glass tinkled on the asphalt. I sat on the hood as Dmitri called 911. I could taste the spaghetti sauce and fruit punch. I thought I was going to puke. I took another drag from my cigarette.

The police, firemen and ambulances didn't take long to show up. Sergeant Hampton, an old family friend who had pulled me over before for other offenses, walked over to me while another officer retraced the tire tracks.

Hey Dughall, how are you? he said.

I didn't respond.

Were you racing tonight?

Yeah, I said.

Do you know how fast were you going when you hit her?

Probably the speed limit. Like 50 or 55.

Okay, have a seat in the car, son.

He pointed to the front seat, I twiddled my thumbs. Breath short. I sat. Sergeant Hampton walked over to Dmitri and said something to him. Dmitri looked at the ground then at me and back to the Sergeant and nodded. Dmitri turned and walked up next to me.

Hey man, he said, I told'em what happened, where you started and everything. We're a good three quarter mile away from the startin line. I think it'll be okay. Your tires have flat spots in'm now. That's how hard you was braking. It wudn't your fault man. Don't worry.

I said nothing. I looked at him, his face calm as he smoked, like we had raced and that was all. In that moment his silence said more than words ever could. I puffed my cigarette. I felt how short life could be as I stared into the warm night. Why did she do this? It was in the mid-seventies and humid but I began shivering. Dmitri patted me on the shoulder and walked away as Sergeant Hampton returned.

Sergeant Hampton silently sat down in the driver's seat. He didn't look at me, but closed his notebook slowly then grasped it tight. He held it with both hands and stared at the steering wheel. The sounds of men talking pushed through the rolled up windows. Red, blue and amber lights flashed across everything. The tall trees and the fields seemed so somber now.

Dughall, he said, I hope this all ends up okay. Right now, minimum, it's likely that your license will be revoked and your car will be towed as evidence. We know your character and know this was unintentional, however, it will not be without consequence. It appears by your long tire marks that you attempted to avoid contact by braking hard and swerving which turned out probably slowed your speed to around forty when you made contact.

We both stared at the floor of the car. I felt a tremble rush through my body, heartbeat quickening.

So what's going to happen? Am I going to jail?

I'm not going to take you in. I've known you and your family too many years. I am going to have to issue you a pretty serious ticket for racing and after reviewing all the evidence, it's possible something more could happen.

He reached over and grabbed my shoulder but I barely noticed.

Son, you ever need to talk, you call me alright?

Okay.

I was relieved that I wouldn't have to worry about jail but an uncomfortable shiver went through my spine. Not fear. Nor awkwardness. But as if my life was instantly different. I had looked death in the eye. And she had stared back with a calmness that I did not understand. I couldn't die that way. It seemed so definitive, frightening. A shiver colder than before crawled across my skull.

Four

The next morning I woke in my apartment and walked to the bedroom window, hopeful I had dreamed it all. My guts rose to my throat when I didn't see the Nova. My heart beat faster. I shook. My lungs felt like I had smoked two packs of cigarettes in a row. My head got light and I nearly passed out. What would happen today? Would police come and arrest me? Voices came from the living room. I felt relieved as I recognized Dmitri's. I walked into the room rubbing my eyes. Dmitri and Frank sprang up, their eyes wide. Dmitri smelled more like alcohol than usual. Frank spoke first.

How are ya man?

Alright. I guess. I'm not really sure.

They both nodded and looked at the floor.

If you need a ride anywhere let me know, said Frank.

I sat down. Dmitri fidgeted with the arm cushion on the couch, kneading it like a cat would their bed. Every minute or so he would take a swig from a flask. Frank stared at the dark TV screen. They were both smoking. I lit a cigarette too.

I'm hungry, I said.

They laughed nervously as if what I had said was inappropriate. I smiled and squirmed in the chair.

We could go to Pancake Town, I'm kinda feeling

some pancakes or waffles, said Frank.

Sounds good, I said.

It was Sunday morning and the restaurant was busy. We waited in the lobby and attempted small talk. Sometimes I would look up and people would be staring at me. I wondered if they were related to that woman. I tried to talk about things that would help me ignore the accident but nothing seemed to make it go away. All I could see was her young, strangely calm face. As if my mind were not enough to irritate me a cop walked in.

Lieutenant Nelson was a family friend, my father had gone to high school and college with him. They had allegedly got into some trouble together with a bowling ball, baseball bat and a mailbox. He was wearing a clean, pressed uniform adorned with shiny pins. A lumpy gun hung from his hip. Our eyes met and he headed toward us.

Hey guys. How are ya today? he said.

Dmitri and Frank shrugged, looking away.

Alright, I said.

The Lieutenant nodded, patting my shoulder.

Dughall, I've got something to tell you if you can step outside for a moment.

I hesitated, positive that I would be arrested. Dmitri's sad eyes soberly told me to face it. Looking at the sea of people in the restaurant, I wanted to run but there was nowhere to go. I bowed my head and followed him out the door.

It was a nice Midwest day. Sun was shining, crisp air drifted and was not too humid or windy. If the race last night had ended normally I would be driving in the country right now.

Dughall, said Lieutenant Nelson, I'm sorry to hear about what happened last night, my prayers are with you. The official police report has stated that it was an accident, but there's a large chance your license will be suspended.

Yeah, that's what Sergeant Hampton said.

I'm telling you this because you have a right to know. If you would like to look at the police report you can. It's all there but they did find out her name and other information if you want to know…

I nodded.

Jessica Hall, she was twenty six. Her family had been looking for her last night after they found a suicide note taped to her bathroom mirror. I thought maybe you would like to know. Not that it justifies what happened but it may help you.

That's horrible. I hope they're doing okay, I said and stood there for a moment before saying, How long will I lose my license?

Depends on the judge. Maybe ninety days, maybe a year.

I looked at the ground as the last twenty-four hours flashed by. Each regret so vivid and avoidable I wished I could relive it the way I wanted it to be. But another feeling rose too. I felt guilty since that lady, Jessica, was dead. What about her family? Why did she have to die that way? What did it all mean?

Look, Dughall, it's not the end of the world. I think your parents would be proud that you tried everything to stop the car before hitting her. Keep your head up and call me if you need anything. Now go back and have some breakfast with your friends.

He smiled as I looked up, putting his hand on my shoulder. I nodded and we shook hands and as I walked back inside he patted my back. Dmitri and Frank must have been seated. I didn't see them when I walked in.

Dughall! Over here! Dmitri was waving from a booth by a window. I walked over and Dmitri asked, What did he want?

He just wanted to tell me some stuff about the accident. I might be losing my license. That girl, her name was Jessica, I guess she was suicidal.

Shit man.

We sat quietly for a moment until Dmitri started talking about how he saw a girl with no underwear sitting across from us. Briefly our familiar juvenile discussions resurfaced but any silence made me think about Jessica Hall. I could see her body pushing away from the car, her eyes looking into mine. I shivered. Dmitri and Frank laughed. Just as we were getting into the conversation again someone said my name. Our faces dropped, aware that whoever it was would inquire about the accident bringing to the forefront what Dmitri and Frank were trying to help me forget.

Dughall!

It was Vicky. She sat down next and said, I tried to get to you last night but the cops wouldn't let me in and I just tried your apartment and no one was home. Drove by here and saw Frank and Dmitri's cars. Are you alright?

I'm alright. Just having breakfast with these two.

I waved my fork at Dmitri and Frank.

I'm so glad you're okay, I was so worried!

Vicky and I were like a brother and sister. We met at fifteen and when we turned sixteen were inseparable. Her boyfriends were always jealous, believing she was cheating on them with me. In truth we would cruise the boulevard, hang out in parking lots with all the other motorheads. We never exchanged a kiss. None of her romantic relationships had lasted, mainly due to their misunderstanding of our relationship. It always surprised me that she stood by me through each one. On this Sunday I was glad she was there.

We walked out of Pancake House, the sun warming our skin, humid air dense, the whoosh of cars on the road filling our ears. I felt my senses heightened, happy to be here. At Vicky's car, she hugged me. The guys looked away. I felt her hand on the back of my head and running her fingers through my hair. She put her hands up to my ears and lowered my head so she could kiss my forehead. She pulled me closer. I could feel her breasts poke my stomach. Her head rested on my chest. She looked up at me, eyes twinkling.

Let's go to a movie or whatever. Let me take you.

Dmitri and Frank had walked over to their cars.

Hey guys, I'm gonna go with Vicky for a while. Thanks for hanging with me this morning.

They nodded and waved.

Five

The hum of the car on the road calmed me. Perhaps it was because Vicky was the most cautious, alert driver I knew. I was glad she wasn't a fast driver. The drive through the country's winding roads was usually a joy, but on that day it was nauseating. I think the only reason I didn't puke was that my senses seemed amplified and I was able to focus on the surroundings. Every tree looked greener, taller than normal. The summer sun shone a brilliant white light and cast across rolling wheat and corn fields. The warm wind blew in the windows, circulating through our hair.

How are you? She said.

It was the first thing either had said since I told her I wanted to go to the river access.

Nervous. I don't know what will happen and I feel horrible about that lady. Lieutenant Nelson was at Pancake House this morning and told me her name was Jessica Hall and she was suicidal. It's all really hard to process.

I can't imagine how frightening it would be. I'm here for you. You know that, right?

Yeah. I know. It sounds selfish too, but I'm scared of losing my license.

It might be selfish if it was your only thought but it's not. You're obviously sad about her too.

Yeah. It's kinda weird too that I'm scared to drive.

I mean, I have no desire to. But I've spent the last five years dedicated to cars and now I don't really want to drive. It's just strange.

She reached over, patted my hand and squeezed it. We continued in silence. Death seemed to be following me. The majority of my teen years had been spent attending funerals. I hoped she wasn't next. She was the closest thing to a family I had since my mom and dad died two years earlier in a car accident and my maternal grandparents passed three years before that. My paternal grandfather died when I five years old and I never met my paternal grandmother. They were gone forever. At each funeral that's all I understood. But it was not the word death or die or even gone that I was beginning to understand. It was the distinctions between each, the reasons and contemplations.

These thoughts buzzed as I stared out at cattle munching grass with no care in the world. Fence posts blurred. The barbwire of the fence remained a constant black line underscored by fescue and weeds. Trees whipped by in hulking brown and white and green. The awareness of movement intensified until I felt like I could puke. I lit a cigarette. Closing my eyes, I breathed in and out as smoke tingled my nostrils.

I opened my eyes and watched as we weaved under large oak trees that looked like the grandfathers of the world. Squirrels jumped across the road. Acorns hit the roof of the car. A hawk flew over. Another sat on top of a utility pole. The lush summer green forest drowned utility poles and gray fences as the warm Midwest river bottom breeze shook tree limbs, bringing the smell of the warm fishy river and earthy forest into the car. I put out the cigarette and inhaled, tasting the humidity. Calm again.

The turn signal clicked, drawing us into the parking lot. Pulling onto the gravel from the asphalt was jarring. It shook the car and rattled the glovebox as we parked. I shut the door, dust rolling around me. I lit another cigarette and walked out to the boat ramp. I could hear Vicky's footsteps behind me. Flip-flops smacking like lips. The boat ramp led to several trails created either by rednecks or game. Much of it required jeans because of all the poison ivy. I stood at the bottom of the ramp watching water caress the concrete. I took a last drag of my cigarette, watching the tongue-like lapping of water inches from my feet. How easy it would be to let it take me away.

I tossed my cigarette toward the parking lot and looked at Vicky and said, You can wait if you want. There's a ton of poison ivy back here.

I'll chance it, she said.

I stepped onto the faded leaf covered trail. Dry leaves crunched. Branches stroked my arms legs and face. The temperature was just right for the cool river wind to mix with the warm humid air. The same feeling you get when you drive down the road with heater on full blast in winter. A peace rose in my chest.

We arrived in the small clearing that looked out onto the river and I felt a great relief more spiritual than emotive. I thought about Jessica. Her eyes locked on mine. I shuddered but felt strangely at peace. Below me the muddy river lapped rocks. A tree branch wavered over the water. Sometimes the wind would blow causing the branch to bob left and right. It would dip briefly into the water as it went to the right, softly spraying droplets out across the fast current. I wondered if Jessica had enjoyed this. Just watching nature.

I tried to imagine what it would be like to have my mother hold me like she used to when I was a child, when she would tell me that it would be okay and somehow hearing her say that would let me know that everything would indeed be okay. I wished my father were here, that silent man who, at the moment I most needed, would ask about the Nova. Tell me what you've done to this thing, he would say. And we would get in the car and drive through the country on winding roads to this river access. Sometimes we would fish here but most times we would sit and watch the river.

Vicky touched my shoulder. She said nothing, hugging me from behind as I watched the water's continuity, forcefully rubbing the shore with its current. She pressed her face and body hard against my back. Her body shook. I held her hands tight against my stomach.

Six

The letter came a week after the accident. My license would be suspended for ninety days. Baumgras had poor bus routes and none came by my apartment. And though it was a small town nobody really walked anywhere because there were very few sidewalks. I had a bicycle somewhere in storage but it was dangerous to ride in Baumgras. A friend of mine in high school, on a dare, had ridden a bicycle on the busiest part of the Boulevard, the main thoroughfare. He did it, rode all the way with cars honking. People waved middle fingers and shouted. We all thought he was nuts. No one ever dared him again. That's how I imagined it would be anywhere I rode a bike in Baumgras.

I didn't want to bother people with my problems so I began to think of the only alternatives I had. I would have to get my bicycle, bum rides or walk. None were especially appealing but I figured a bicycle would be the best choice. I knew I would need something to keep me occupied. But until I found my bike, I needed to get my life together. I had gone to a technical school when I graduated high school but had dropped after a semester. Maybe now was the time to go back.

College had been something my father had wanted for me. He had never been to college and thought I deserved to go. Mom always talked about college and how fun it had been but she never used her degree because she stayed home with me. The accident made it seem like I needed to fulfill The American Dream. Fulfill their dream for my life. Get an education. Find a girl. Get a good paying job. Get married. My dad would have been upset when I quit going. I decided that at least in my father's memory I should give it one more try. I walked to the community college down the street from my apartment to register for night classes.

The building smelled like fresh paint and plaster. It was clean and roomy. In front of the office, students sat at desks filling out paperwork, doing homework. I walked up to the window trying not to stare at the girl on the other side of the window. She was gorgeous. Red hair. Full lips. A little cleavage showing.

Hi, how can I help you?

I need to see about registering.

She smiled a very large smile. It made me squirm.

She took down my name and as she paged an adviser I noticed on her left hand a large sparkling ring. My heart sank. She looked and smiled again as she hung up the phone. Her lips rubbed together as if she had just applied chapstick or lipstick. She motioned me back to an office.

If you would like to come back and have a seat in Nancy's office. She will be with you shortly.

She brushed her hair over her shoulder and lingered for a moment staring at me. Eyes gentle. Calm.

Reminded me of Jessica Hall. I felt a chill as she turned. Red hair swished. Skirt hugged her ass. Calves flexed in high heels. I sat down and leaned over slightly. Closed my eyes for a moment only to relive Jessica's stare through the windshield of the Nova. I shuddered. Opened my eyes.

The office was nothing spectacular. Glimpses of the adviser's personal life. Pictures, diploma and awards. There was a large motivational poster in the room. Black border with an elephant and mouse in the center. A cheesy slogan read, Only you can be large enough to believe you can move a mountain.

Dughall?

The adviser walked in. Short. Round. Middle aged.

Yeah.

Hi, I'm Carol Pendleton. What can I help you with today? What are you interested in studying?

Creative writing and history. I really like poetry but there's probably no degree for that . . .

No . . . not here anyway. We have an option for history though. Would that be something you are interested in?

Her words sounded as if I was supposed to choose something else, something more noble. The rest of the conversation was mundane and I dissociated, though it's hard to say which came first. I daydreamed somehow maintaining an understanding of the conversation. I dreamed about everything. The accident. The redhead receptionist. Drunken high school nights in open fields enjoying the company of others, yet alone. Our conversation quickly came to an end.

Well since we don't have a creative writing program, I think the best bet for you is to get you enrolled in a Bachelor of Arts program in History. You can always change that later if you wish, she said.

Okay.

I could tell she wanted to say something else. Her eyes stuck on me for a moment. Mouth opened but nothing came out. She ducked down close to her desktop.

I'm sorry to hear about the accident.

Thanks.

You know, I don't know if you've talked to the family but my husband had a similar accident almost twenty years ago and he wrote the family a letter. He said just writing it made him feel better. But despite that, the family has kept up correspondence with him all these years. We even exchange Christmas cards each year. Oh well, I feel like I'm preachin now. I was just so sorry to hear that this happened and I put two and two together when I saw your name just now. I sure hope you're doing okay Dughall. We're glad to have you. Keep your chin up.

I left her office in a hazy dream, the whole world toppling. Jessica Hall was everywhere. Even women I was attracted to reminded me of her. My head swelled and ached with life's ever present radiance and sorrow. I sat outside on a bench in the sun and chain-smoked. After thirty minutes I called Dmitri and told him I was coming over. He said his sister Cari had been asking about me. I could tell he was drunk and I didn't ask him to pick me up. I smiled as I hung up and called Frank for a ride.

Seven

Frank picked me up and explained that he couldn't stay long. He had to be at work early in the morning. Truth was, Frank didn't like being around Dmitri when he was drunk. He said he reminded him of his father who used to beat him and his sister when they were growing up. Frank tolerated Dmitri when they were in town but out at Dmitri's place Frank rarely stuck around.

Dmitri lived twenty miles out of town on some land he had bought with graduation money and selling meth. His trailer was nice but I rarely went inside. He considered the outdoors the restroom, bedroom and storage facility. Like any good redneck, which he claimed he was, he only asked that you cover your shit. We pulled in hoping he wasn't completely wasted. Frank wasn't going to get out so I thanked him and jumped out. I looked over to see Dmitri taking a piss next to the Trans Am. He turned toward me, still peeing.

Holy shit! It's the man of the hour! Welcome home, Dughall.

He zipped up, walked toward me, topless, arms outstretched holding a Natural Light beer can.

Hey Dmitri what's up?

Nothin man, waitin for you guys to get here to get this party started! Frank, get outta the car, stay a while!

Nah. I gotta get up early.

Aw man c'mon. Just have a few.

Sorry but I'll have to pass. See you guys later.

Frank nodded to me as he put the Charger in reverse and backed out onto the street. The mellow hollow sound of the Mopar engine roared as his rear tires belched smoke.

Dmitri cheered, Goddam, that car can fry the tires. Fuckin shit!

He took a swig from his can and nodded toward the trailer. I followed the nod. Cari walked out, a smile on her face. She held a cigarette and a wine cooler. I stuck up my hand in a motionless wave. She walked over and gave me tight hug. Her flowery vanilla perfume wafted through my nostrils. Cari was two years older than me and would graduate with a marketing degree in December. Ever since I had been hanging out with Dmitri, Cari had been nearby. I never thought it would go any further. But one night when I was eighteen it did.

We had stayed awake watching Days of Heaven. It was her favorite movie at the time. Dmitri quickly fell asleep after drinking a beer and smoking a joint. She scooted over to sit by me when he did. The side of her butt touched mine. Her hand found its way into my pants. We got up, her hair cradled her cheeks. Bottom lip partially concealed by her front teeth. She knelt so her face was level with mine. I smelt fruity shampoo and felt her hair tickle my neck. Her lips brushed mine. It was barely a kiss.

Follow me, she said and grabbed the neck of my shirt and dragged me into her bedroom.

What if your parents hear?

They won't.

She motioned for me to sit down on the bed as she took off her bra and shirt. Kissing my forehead and gently pushing my chest I fell back. She straddled my crotch with hers. She kissed my lips hard. I felt her tongue inside my mouth. Breasts pressed against my chest, her crotch on mine. My lips grew numb. This memory struck me as she pulled away from our embrace. Our eyes met. Hers twinkled.

Ya'll wanna go muddin? Dmitri said.

Cari nodded and I said, Let's do it man.

As we climbed into the tall truck Cari pretended to struggle with the height. I was behind her and she asked me to pick her up. I held her by the waist but before I lifted her up she reached between my legs grabbing my privates. They tingled. I hoisted her up and jumped in behind her. I prayed Dmitri didn't look over as I sat down. I had a boner. As I sat down I took off my hat and put it between my legs.

Damn man you're always wearin that hat. You alright?

Cari giggled. I jabbed her ribs lightly.

Umm…yeah, just kinda got a headache.

Aww shit, sorry man.

31

He fired up the truck and let out the clutch, beer in his lap. We drove on gravel roads for an hour or so briefly breaking off the trail to splash through a creek or take a leak. Occasionally Cari would rub my leg. As with any back road mudding expedition I've ever been on, the mundane gravel-roading and minor mudding always had a giant climax. We stopped in the middle of the dark dusty road. Dmitri took another sip. The air was thick as if we were about to go to war.

Hold on, kids. This'll be a ride.

The truck roared turning suddenly toward what looked like trees but as we left the gravel road we dropped off onto a trail. Bouncing. Sliding. Flinging mud.

Goddam, hold on. Here it comes!

As soon as Dmitri said it muddy water came from everywhere. Goopey gooey mud. The tires thrashed the wet ground. We went slow now. Engine roaring. Tires grabbing for anything to try to pull us out. Dmitri rapidly turned the steering wheel back and forth hoping to find some traction. Slowly the truck crept out, smelling of hot metal and oil. Dmitri shut off the truck and jumped out pointing at the side of the truck.

Woohoo! That was the mudhole from hell! Look how deep that shit was! I gotta take a piss.

Cari slightly lowered her head and looked at me.

When we get back, you wanna hang out?

Sure, I said.

Eight

Dmitri jumped back into the cab. Cari told him she was ready to go to the trailer. He drove erratically all the way back, making me glad we would be retiring for the night. He was wasted. When we got there, Dmitri almost immediately fell asleep in the bed of his truck. Cari grabbed my hand and walked toward the trailer.

Are you hungry?

Yeah I could eat.

I've got some leftovers.

Excited, though a bit uncomfortable I went inside. I rarely ever went in the trailer. It smelled like stale popcorn. The lights were dim but I could see clothes strewn across the couch and floor of the living room. Despite the disarray it had a sort of homey feel to it, mostly because Cari stayed here often. It was definitely not something I would expect from Dmitri. Cari squatted on the floor, quietly riffling through the refrigerator. Her butt was heart-shaped nearly squeezing out of her pants.

So, looks like we've got leftover macaroni casserole or I could make you a bologna sandwich. What do you think?

I'd go with the casserole.

Cari was uncharacteristically quiet. Her forehead furrowed and her teeth bit her lower lip, her mouth moved side to side while waiting on the food to heat up. She stared blankly at the countertops making me feel like I could have left without her knowledge. As she pulled my plate out of the microwave I could tell she was on the verge of saying something.

Wanna beer?

I nodded.

Her lips moved apart the same way the counselor's had. She looked at me seriously handing me the plate. I took it.

So . . . how are you doing? Her tone was somber. Concerned. I knew she was referring to the accident.

Okay I guess. Just still shook up I think. I can't get this vision of her out of my head. It just lingers. Especially at night when I'm trying to sleep. I see her coming toward me like some demon in a horror film. Except it really happened. And sometimes . . . it sounds silly but sometimes I think I see her standing in my room when all the lights are out.

She lit a cigarette and stared out the window. I followed her lead. Neither of us touched our food. She exhaled and set her cigarette on the ashtray.

I think that's natural Dughall. You're thinking about it. If you weren't scared or disturbed in some way I'd say there's something wrong. But that's not how it is. And you're thinking it through. I think you're doing good with what you've got to deal with.

I guess so. I've been trying to handle it all by

myself and maybe that's a problem. I'm not really sure. I'm trying to figure out the right way but maybe there is no right way. It's all just up to me. I just wanted to live this life how I wanted and all I wanted was to drive. And now I can't. I don't have a license and I'm actually afraid to. It scares me what I would see or experience.

My eyes teared up and I lowered my head hoping she wouldn't notice. I felt her soft fingers touch the top of my hand. I looked over at her. She nodded and smiled.

We ate in the silent melancholy of heavy conversation. I felt an uneasiness that I should feel uncomfortable in this silence. These topics were large in scope for only eating casserole. But it felt good to talk about it. It felt good to have Cari listen. I hadn't allowed myself to let go like that. I perceived that no one wanted to talk about death, they only wanted the pleasantries and niceties of caring but not the entire truth. But maybe this wasn't true. It wasn't that way with Cari.

Dughall . . . I maybe should've asked you this before, but do you want to go out sometime?

I finished my last bite of casserole hoping it would help think of the perfect response.

Yeah, sure, that'd be fun.

I sounded like an idiot but she nodded in approval. I saw a smile form as she turned to put the dishes in the sink. Returning to the table she took my hand and led me to the bedroom she called hers. I took off my

35

clothes and got in bed. She disrobed and crawled up. I looked at her body. Small breasts. Perky nipples. I took her hand pulling her to my chest. Her hair warmly embraced my shoulder and neck. I didn't want sex tonight. I just wanted this. We lay there and her hand rose resting on my chest. Her body relaxed and breathing changed and mine followed. Before I drifted away I kissed her head.

Nine

The smell of bacon and eggs and coffee saturated the air. I got dressed. Cari was cooking in the kitchen. Dmitri sat at the dining table drinking a can of cheap beer. His face brightened as I walked out.

Hey stud. Sleep good?

Cari shot him a quick glare.

Yeah, slept fine. Hair of the dog?

He smiled, raising his beer in a cheers. Cari sighed as she plopped bacon onto our plates.

You need to quit drinking so much. You're going to end up an alcoholic like grandpa was, Cari said.

Nah. I'll quit when I'm thirty. Our twenties are for partying, right Dughall? Have a beer buddy.

He held up an unopened can.

I'll pass. Maybe later, I said.

That's cool, one more for me.

Dmitri! What if mom came to visit right now? She would be pissed!

He shrugged and with a slight smile grabbed his two beers and walked outside. Cari stood still for a moment. She picked up the bacon from one of the plates opened the door and chucked them outside as if she were sowing seeds or feeding chickens.

Fuck you Dmitri! I just don't want you to get in any trouble!

The door slammed. Her face flushed red. I had seen them argue before but her reaction this time seemed more heartfelt, more emotional. She finished making breakfast, setting his plate of eggs and hash browns aside she brought our plates over and ate. A cautious tense silence followed. I didn't speak. I was glad when I heard her soft tired voice.

I just want him to be okay Dughall. I watched grandpa die. It was painful. And I don't want him to go through that but he just doesn't listen.

Do your parents know?

I think they suspect but I don't think they know. They hardly come here and Dmitri only goes home when he's sober. He's clever that way. I could talk to them about it but I don't think that would have any lasting positive effect on him. It would probably make him worse.

Because he would rebel?

She nodded. I scooted my chair over and hugged her. Her face buried in my shoulder I felt the weight of the situation. What was this adulthood? Maybe Dmitri was right in living his way. Cari and I held each other tight. My shoulder grew wet and in this embrace, I saw Jessica Hall. She stood behind us her face spread open in a scream. I closed my eyes and buried my head in Cari's shoulder.

Cari took me to work shortly after. And we kissed like an old couple when she dropped me off. Soft. Brief. Tender. I wanted to stay with her. It made me sad to see her drive away. The rest of the day I thought about her. My hands gripped ratchets and wrenches. Extracting bolts. Draining fluids. It was all automatic. A trance. I saw only Cari. I looked down at my hands covered in black sticky grease. How could anyone love these hands?

Ten

On my lunch break I walked on white shimmering concrete. Heat waves floated in the distance. The Midwest air felt like breathing hot vapor from a paper bag but I hardly noticed. Cari's eyes and lips and hair were all I could see. I took out my cell phone. I fidgeted with the buttons. It kept ringing. I waited for her voice to say hello. It didn't. I hung up.

I walked back to work. I guess she didn't like me after all. She knew it was me and ignored the call. I kicked a rock. Watched it skitter into the street. I looked up to see Jessica. I did not feel fear this time. I just wanted her to quit haunting me. I ran toward the vision.

What do want from me? I said.

She opened her mouth as if beginning to speak but then vanished. Was she real? Was I hallucinating? Why was she bothering me like this? She was the one who wanted to die. I instantly felt guilty for this last thought. I prayed though I wasn't sure if there was anything to pray to. I asked for forgiveness. I was glad I had work when I got back. I focused my energy on cold metal moving parts the rest of the afternoon.

Vicky picked me up from work. My mind was still processing the emotions of the day when I got in the car. Pop music was on the radio. The woman's voice shrieked. I wanted to yank her from the music studio and smash the microphone. I didn't want to hear this right now. I hoped Vicky would somehow read my mind and turn it off.

How was your day? Vicky said

Not the greatest.

Vicky reached over and turned off the radio and said, Tell me about it.

Do you ever feel like someone is watching you? Like from the grave?

She nodded slowly as we pulled into the street.

Well, it's weird but I've seen that lady. The lady I hit. I've seen her twice in the last twenty-four hours.

Seen her how? Like a ghost?

Yeah I guess so. It's like she's following me. I should be happy today but I keep seeing her. This morning Jessica showed up behind Cari. It was freaky. She stood just looking over her shoulder with that final frightened look on her face. Then this afternoon I saw her on the street. It's scaring the shit out of me Vicky. I don't know what to do.

Maybe you should talk to somebody about it. You went to that one therapist after your parents died. Why don't you go back to her?

She moved to Texas I think. I don't know if she would've been any help anyway. She probably would've put me on some anti-psychotic medication or something.

Maybe. You could hold a séance or something.

Forget it.

I said nothing else. I just wanted the visions to stop. I wanted to live my life. Enjoy this time with Cari. I was hopeful about this relationship. I'd always been dedicated to cars before and never really had a solid romantic relationship. Most girls had left or I had left them. I had been too aloof or too dedicated to my car. I let them go. But now seemed to be the right time to try.

Me and Cari are going on a date soon.

Like an official date? Oh how exciting!

I nodded.

You're finally settling down? Tell me all about it.

I feel a lot with her. I guess I always have but she kinda opened it up to the next level last night. She asked if I wanted to go out sometime.

I'm so excited for you! You two will make such a great couple.

Maybe I expected her to be my therapist. But she had said nothing profound. I assumed the topic was too dark and she just wanted to avoid it and waving away my anxiety by offering other options. None of them appealed to me. Perhaps I subconsciously wanted to vanquish this anxiety, to confront that which frightened me and show the ghost of Jessica Hall that my strength was stronger than her persistence.

Vicky hugged me before I walked to my apartment. On the way up I checked my phone. Maybe somehow I had missed Cari's return phone call. I thumbed through my outgoing calls looking at my call to her a few times before throwing the phone down on the couch. Cari must not really want to go out. She had just been drunk and tried to make me feel better. I lit a cigarette and grabbed a six pack from the fridge.

Eleven

Halfway through my fourth beer and twice as many cigarettes, Cari called. I let it ring twice.

Hey Cari.

I'm so sorry I didn't call you earlier. I had to meet up with a few people after school to go over this project we're working on. I miss you. How was your day?

I imagined telling her of my misdirected anger from not hearing from her. Or that I kept having unpleasant visions of Jessica Hall or that I had been drinking to forget this entire day. But I didn't.

It was good. Thought about you a lot.

Aww . . . you're sweet.

How was your project?

Good. It was for this marketing class I'm taking. It's actually pretty fun.

You're majoring in marketing right?

No. Business Administration. You're going back to school too, right?

Yeah. Decided on history.

That should be interesting.

We talked for a couple more hours and arranged a formal date for Friday night. I hung up feeling drunk but not on the beer.

We decided to eat downtown. For some reason I told her that the Italian restaurant Rafino's could be good but I would think about it further. I couldn't think of another place. Stomach queasy, twirling upside down with nervous hunger I thought about the situation. What to say what to wear what quirks and ticks should I terminate? All week nervousness took precedence.

She showed up at my door. Black and white dress. Strands of her hair indistinguishable, all flowing as one soft pillow. Eyes sparkled. Lips pursed and puffed. She looked so sexy, too good for me.

Where'd you decide to eat?

Is Rafino's okay?

That's fine with me. Are you really okay with eating there? I mean I know you said Italian food doesn't sit well with you after . . .

It's okay, I'm fine with it.

The restaurant was busy when we got there. Thirty minute wait. Sitting down at a bench outside she held my hand. We allowed silence as the sunset bloomed. Orange pink smeared clouds. People walked past, conversing or nervously denying our existence. We created our own comfortable world. After five minutes she smiled and squeezed my hand.

What else do you like to do other than work on cars and race?

I don't know. I've actually been thinking a lot about that lately. It's always been my life. An escape I guess. But I think I might start drawing and writing poetry again. I used to draw and paint before I started driving. And I've always written poetry.

I love poetry. I'd love to read some of yours.

It's not very good.

I'm sure it is.

The hostess called our name and seated us. We ordered drinks and entrees filling time with small talk about menu options and what we could eat.

So what kind of poetry do you write? Do you have common topics you tend to write about? Cari said.

I write a lot about nature or love, I said.

I'd really like to read it! Will you let me sometime?

Of course. What kind of poetry do you like?

Love and nature are favorites. I'm into darker poetry too. I really like Emily Dickinson and Poe.

Yeats has some good dark poetry too. I like Whitman and Emerson for nature poetry.

Oooh yes, I love both of them.

Have you read any Gary Snyder?

Yes! I just picked up Turtle Island the other day and read a little of it.

I love Turtle Island. The poem called I Went into the Maverick Bar is amazing.

That's a great poem.

It's one of my favorites right now. What about you? What's your favorite poem?

Ugh, it's hard to pick just one but I really like, I

Hide Myself Within Your Flower by Emily Dickinson.

That's a good one. I didn't have any idea you were so into poetry.

Likewise.

She smiled and looked up at me as she took a sip of water. Our conversation flowed now. Walking out we held hands. Righteous comfort suspended in the night amid other lovers, old and new, all sharing the same experience. The electric fantastic euphoria of love declared, announced in interlocked fingers, wide wondering eyes and tender full kisses. We stopped under a garden's vine woven trellis and the moon smiled. Our eyes held the tenderness and forgetfulness of everything as we kissed the kiss the whole world knows.

Twelve

We made love when we got to my apartment but I had a hard time sleeping afterward. Cari on my mind. I lay next to her as she slept. Her breath deep, nearly snoring. My heart pounded. Thoughts wandered to high school and a guy who had been in my French class. I never really talked to him but he had a way with people. He always made them laugh. On a Monday morning we heard he had been in a serious accident and was brain dead.

The counselor came to our class and told anyone if they needed to talk she was there. I never went but maybe I should have. I should have at least talked with my therapist about it. I remember him sitting in class laughing and talking. His face vivid as the day I last saw him. Sometimes I think I should have died in his place. He was hopeful, happy. Made people laugh. I wish I had that gift.

I saw his girlfriend Harmony crying in front of school a few days after the accident. I had wanted to comfort her but thought it would've been weird since she didn't know me. I wanted to make her feel better somehow, tell her it was alright and that life will go on and all the same inconsequential things everyone had told me after my parents' accident.

And now I wish that he could be here instead, that she never would've cried for him. I wanted instead to be with my parents and grandparents who had disappeared in the last five years. They never would've needed to cry for me. I would've felt less guilty knowing everyone in my family had passed on quickly after me. Instead I can still see Harmony's face with its streaked make-up and her sour lips. She reminded me of Jessica. They had the same build.

Jessica Hall. What would cause her to commit suicide? Twenty-six years old. Why would she do that? I looked over at Cari for comfort. I wanted her to take me. Press my head to her breasts. I thought of waking her but she lay so peaceful. I got up for a cigarette, grabbed a beer on the way to the deck.

Opening the sliding door, the street lamps looked like candles, their light not passing much farther than the street. Above the deck, the moonlight shone between the hovering trees. Everything silent. After midnight in a small town it feels that way. Nothing moves. A late night summer breeze tugged my shirt, fluttered my hair. I feel alone. I don't want to be. Not now. I want someone to comfort me. But I stand. Alone. As I have thousands of times before. Smoking a cigarette under the howling despondent sky.

I toss the half empty beer bottle onto the apartment's lawn. Jessica Hall must have felt this. This loneliness. Maybe she felt a fearful wanderlust. Trapped in this life. Maybe she saw each decision as a mistake. Her entire life degraded by each tiny indiscretion. Each person she walked casually by and though inclined, never spoke to. Each right turn should've been a left. Revealing a hidden journey leading away from where she was now. It all made sense. I toss my cigarette butt toward the bottle.

I woke to Cari kissing my forehead.

I'm going shopping with my mom. See you later.

Later.

Her face stared at mine. I wanted her to stay. She left. I wanted something new. Some sort of happiness. There was nothing. Usually I would drive away from it. Instead I went for a walk. Daydreaming of driving until the highway becomes two lanes and winds, weaving around farms and fields. The smell of asphalt and tar replaced with the moist lush smell of vegetation. Farm houses and barns scattered far apart, secluded just enough to make the inhabitants feel alone. The corn and wheat fields magnify this too with their vast green and tan emptiness. Bobwhites. Whippoorwills. Grasshoppers. Crickets. Crows. All unify to serenade me as I envision stumbling upon old homesteads. Grey crumbling masses hidden under rusting roofs.

I could see Cari and I holding hands, picturesque and timeless. She holds a camera, snaps a shot of me. I would stroll across the dirt drive. Pen in hand. Writing poetry. I breathe in the corn and wheat winds and imagine laying in the hay with Cari, on our backs sharing only slow time. Watching the colors change as the sun sets.

Thirteen

It was almost September. College would start soon and I was nervous. A week before classes began Vicky and I drove out to Dmitri's trailer to meet up with Cari. As usual Dmitri was pretty lit when we got there.

Gettin square on us ain't you Dughall?

Nah. Just decided it's time to move on from high school. Learn something new.

Shit! All I need to know is what's at the bottom of a keg. Yessir that's all I need.

You drink too much man.

Fuck I do! You need to drink more. C'mon! Vicky you'll join me right?

He tossed her a beer without waiting for a nod. She smiled at him and handed me the can. I opened it and took a swig.

No Dmitri, I don't really like beer all that much. It tastes like pee.

Well hot damn Vicky, I don't know what to say. It's the goddam best tasting piss I've ever had! What the hell you gonna be studyin Dughall? Some preppy bullshit?

History or literature.

Aw fuck. You are goin square.

Nah. I wouldn't do that man.

I had hoped to get a chuckle from him but he was too cynical. The air was thick. Vicky fidgeted. Cari pulled into the drive. Vicky rushed up to her car and whispered something to Cari. They walked over, wrinkled brows.

Hey Dughall, Cari said kissing me lightly on the forehead. She smiled a thin tired smile at me before looking at Dmitri.

Dmitri? You okay? You need to take a nap?

Dmitri wobbled. His eyes tried to focus.

I wanna go fuckin drive aroun. Les go muddin!

I don't think that'd be a good idea. Let's go inside, Cari said as she put a hand on his back.

Fuck off!

Dmitri shrugged her hand away and threw his hat on the ground. Cari said something softly to him. Something we could not hear. Dmitri pulled his cell phone out of his pocket and flung it against a tree. It shattered. I walked toward them but Dmitri stormed into the trailer, slamming the door behind him. I'd never seen him this drunk and angry before. Cari walked down to me.

Is he going to be alright? Vicky asked.

He'll be fine. I've never seen him that bad before. Have you ever seen him that way Dughall?

I shook my head and said, No. The closest he came to that was in high school at a party when this guy kept jabbing Dmitri in the ribs for no reason. Dmitri had looked over at me and said, He does that again I'm gonna fuckin clock him. The guy jabbed him again and Dmitri turned around, looked the guy in the face and said, Happy birthday punk. And punched him right on the nose. The guy dropped his beer and ran off. Dmitri looked at me again and said, Let's have another beer! That guy never bothered him again. But Dmitri didn't even look or sound that angry then.

He just needs to quit drinking. But, ugh, alright! Where are we going? Cari said.

Let's go bowling or play pool or something. Are you game Vicky? I said, turning to Vicky.

She glanced back at the trailer.

Are you sure he'll be okay? I mean he's not going to hurt himself right?

Cari stopped and put a hand on Vicky's shoulder and said, He's going to be fine. He'll just go to sleep and won't wake up for hours. Trust me.

Cari and Vicky embraced, sharing emotions in the way people do when they are worried. Cari motioned to me and I walked over joining them. I closed my eyes as I felt both their hands on my back.

Fourteen

It was autumn. Orange and yellow and red leaves hung from trees covering streets and sidewalks. College had started and I had gone part time at the garage. Cari and I spent as much time together as we could but in those times between it became lonely. Dmitri was rarely in a condition to pick me up and had been kicked out of the volunteer fire department. He was boozing more than ever. Maybe he was having visions like I was.

I had begun seeing her nearly every day. I would roll over, close my eyes and reopen them to see Jessica. Mouth agape arms outstretched towards me. I never told Cari but would pull her close. Desiring to take her with me should I be banished from this life. Sometimes Jessica would appear in the morning while eating breakfast, paying me no mind. Other times I would see her as I rode my bike through town, she walking across the street in front of me. Staring.

I felt true sadness toward her. I wish I could change it all. But I felt more than simple sadness or compassion. It was an embodiment of life itself. I wanted to give it back to her. The yearning aroused me. Dug under my skin like a hungry maggot trying to tell me there was more than this experience. The meaning of the accident was intertwined with my own growth and though I wish Jessica were alive I understand it had to be.

I decided to write a letter to Jessica Hall's family. I hadn't done anything for them. I had been too frightened. I sat down with pen and paper and wrote.

> Dear Hall Family,
>
> I am sorry for your loss. I truly wish there was something I could do to bring Jessica back. Instead, I can only voice my sorrow. As I write this letter, words are difficult. I sit here wondering what happened on that day. Why did it have to happen, what was its purpose? I cannot answer these questions, but I wish all the pain and confusion would just leave for all of us. All I want is to go back and change it all. Please know that I am truly sorry and saddened by your loss.
>
> – Dughall Martin

I let the letter fall into the mailbox, fluttering until it hit the bottom. I started walking back to the apartment and wished I hadn't mailed it. Maybe my words sounded foolish. Naïve. Maybe it wasn't perfect enough, but it was too late to retrieve it now. I went back to my apartment and sat down on the couch. I looked at where Cari hung her keys. It was Sunday and she was away doing school work with her business group. Dmitri wasn't answering his phone and Frank was out of town with his family and Vicky was on a date.

I looked over at my mountain bike. Thick knotty tires protruding from the geometric perfect lines of the frame. Raw jagged gears hid behind aluminum pedals. The bike had rapidly replaced the Nova. I checked and cleaned the gears every other evening. Sometimes I would polish the black paint to a smooth sheen. I knew I needed to ride.

A wet early autumn rain lingered on decaying leaves on the trail. The bike slipped around corners and made me wish I would've brought my helmet. At first my skin was cool, my chest anxious, worried that these visions of Jessica were insanity. That they would lead to the destruction of me and Cari's relationship and my own destruction. The activity of the ride thrust a comforting warmth on skin and mind. Calm steady vision of the trail evolved from anxiety.

Concrete asphalt gave way to mud. The trail was unauthorized by city officials and I had found it by chance. Unlevel muddy ground met tires. Tires grabbed sometimes sliding in goopey clay-like mud. Bunny-hopping over fallen limbs the bike landed as if on a cushion. I pedaled faster. Mud flung onto my back and legs and face. Meeting asphalt again, the tires launched chunks of wet debris. Electric euphoria rattled through me. I felt for a moment invincible. Alive.

Fifteen

I locked the bike up outside. Its frame filthy. Splattered with chunks of dark and light brown. Cari was in the apartment.

Did you forget what tomorrow was? she said.

Monday?

You get your license back!

I forgot I guess, I said.

Are you excited?

I'm kind of nervous. I'm not sure how I'll handle driving. I still get nervous when I see people walking near the road and at night. I just don't know. I don't know if that's who I am anymore.

The words felt whispered. Mysterious. Disconnected. Cari stared at me.

Maybe you should get a different car. Another one, you know?

I've thought about that. Maybe something that gets better gas mileage.

She nodded, looking at the floor. My nervousness returned. Maybe she was embarrassed to have brought it up. Maybe I embarrassed her. I looked out the window at the Nova. Gray primered hood and roof and trunk. Simple lines of the muscle car era. The new windshield shone and reflected the front of the building. Dmitri had put it in a few weeks ago. Frank had switched out my tires. Every week they would start it and drive it. I never rode with them. The car had once given me peace and pride. That was not so now. It seemed so long ago.

Should I sell it?

Cari's face dropped. Probably shocked I could ask such a question. Wondering why and how I could sell the closest thing I had to a child.

Dughall . . . why don't you keep it? Maybe you'll want to drive it again someday.

I don't know if I can. I can't even get the courage to sit in it let alone drive it.

You could park it at my parents or Dmitri's. They wouldn't care. Why don't you just wait and see?

I didn't say anything else. The light from the sun exposed tiny shadowy crevices on the low pile carpet. Cari's feet slipped in and out of her shoes. My own bare feet grew warm as the sun shifted position. What she said was not an option. I had to sell it. The decision seemed more final on Monday when I bought a paper. Thumbing through lines of used cars. Classics. Trucks. Cars. It had to be the perfect one. Something with a bit of performance. Definitely sporty. Not too feminine. Seven year old Camaro. It was perfect. Cari and I went and looked at it. Buying it on the spot. We drove to show Dmitri.

Goddam Dughall! Goin modern! Never thought I'd see this day.

I chuckled and said, I'm thinking of selling the

Nova. Know anyone that'd be interested?

Shit man. I don't know right off. I'll ask around.

I kinda hoped you'd be interested in it?

Nah. I couldn't afford it for one. Two, I could never own that car. It was yours. It'd be like dating a girlfriend after one of your buddies. It just ain't right.

It had been a difficult decision and I had hoped Dmitri would buy her. I understood his dilemma. Cari pleaded with me not to sell but I listed the Nova and sold it before the week was over. Steve Garard, a guy from St. Louis picked her up. My heart sank as he drove her away on his trailer. I hoped someday I would see her again.

Sixteen

After I sold the Nova the visions of Jessica largely disappeared. Winter came and during the days I worked at the garage. Oily skin. Bloody knuckles. At night, pen or pencil in hand I listened to lectures on history and literature and writing. Most nights I just wanted to leave and go see Cari. I would sit in class dreaming of her soft fruit scented hair. Her eyes and skin. I would go to the apartment and we would talk about leaving Baumgras. Her head would lay on my lap as we sat on the couch. I would sift her hair softly.

She would say, You know, I've always wanted to go to Oregon. I hear it's gorgeous. Or California. Big Sur has always intrigued me. We should go sometime. Can we?

Her bottom lip would bite her upper and I would smile and nod.

We have to go to both beaches too! The east and west coast and even the Gulf. I want to see it all. Can we? Can we?

Yes, I would say.

And we would sleep, tangled in a naked mass, our hands touching the other as we would fall asleep.

One Saturday morning after such a night, Vicky called. It was the first time I had talked to her in a few weeks. Her biology studies had become intense and I had been busy with work and school and Cari. Her voice was full of excitement and wanted to stop by. Cari had left to have brunch with her mother and I told her to stop by. She had a smile on her face when I opened the door.

She gave me a hug and said, Dughall it's been so long since I've talked to you! I have so much to tell you.

Yeah likewise. So what's going on?

I've been dating this guy Brent who I met through a girl in my biology class. He's so wonderful! I hope you can meet him soon. We're getting pretty serious and talking about what to do after college. He graduates in the spring and I think I'm going to move in with him. He's moving back to St. Louis where his parents live.

I sat. Surprised. Vicky had never been a very spontaneous person. She wasn't the kind of girl to move away from family.

Congratulations. I'll miss you. I'd like to meet him soon though. Maybe a double date with Cari and I?

She gave an excited shiver. Smile stuck on her face. We sat for a moment. Her hands retreated to the zipper on her coat. She moved it up and down before she said, You know I . . .

Cari walked in holding an envelope. Her face cheerful. Excited.

Dughall, this letter was in the mailbox, she said as she handed it to me. The return address simply read, Hall. The girls said nothing as I ripped open the letter. I pulled out the sheet of paper that was carefully folded in thirds.

My hands shook. I sat down on the couch between the girls and began reading.

> Dear Dughall,
> This is Carla Hall, Jessica's mother. My family is heartbroken. We know you didn't mean to hit our girl and it wasn't your fault. But there is some sadness we have that the law didn't do more. Our girl died in an accident and there were no repercussions. We appreciate your words but I think it would be best to not talk further.
> – Carla Hall

I put the letter on my knee. I looked for some ancient code. Hoped it was a joke. A lie. Something false. Cari's hand rubbed the back of my head. I nearly didn't feel it. I felt out of body. Alone. I didn't want them there. I only wanted to think and stew on her words.

Seventeen

Vicky left soon after I opened the letter. Cari rubbed my back as the door closed. I opened and refolded the letter, never reading it again but catching glimpses as I fidgeted.

Dughall, are you going to be okay?

I shrugged.

Would it help to maybe talk to someone?

Nah, I just need some time to myself.

We sat there and she rubbed my head and ran her fingers gently up and down my back.

Maybe I should start writing poetry again, I said.

Cari was silent for a moment and then said, You should if you want to. I would love it if you did. I think it could help.

I nodded. I had been writing poetry since I was twelve. But this was different. There was something new about this desire to write. It felt necessary and as I sat there with Cari, I thought of all the months I had not written anything. And I felt empty. Like it had all been a waste of life.

In the mornings before work I would wake earlier to write a new poem each day. Sometimes on my lunch break I would write. And in class too I would write. When Cari was not at my apartment and I was alone, that's all I did. I wrote poetry and poetic prose essays. It was therapy and I began to feel more at ease. But though several of the poems were about Cari, I had a hard time showing her. She asked to see them but I only showed her my early poetry which she said she enjoyed.

I was also nervous to show anyone else what I had written. Much of it was dark. Depressing. And from what I knew of writing, this didn't appeal to the majority of people. But I also knew I needed approval from someone. It would never come if I didn't share. I thought of connecting with other authors. Writers. I thought of sharing with my English Composition teacher. I did not. Each time I thought about sharing, a great anxiety rose like heartburn. I feared rejection.

But in early spring, Vicky, Brent, Frank and Dmitri came over to my apartment for a barbeque. The evening began normally. Cari hung on my arm. Dmitri chugged through half a case of beer. Frank smoked cigarettes while he barbequed. Vicky told us about their plans. It was the first time I had met Brent. He stood in the background. Not talking unless asked a question. He was thin. Glasses. Looked like he was into science. He looked out of place. The end of the night neared. Dmitri passed out on the couch and Vicky announced they would leave soon.

Before we go, we've got an announcement, she said and glanced at Brent who gave a calm smile. Her face flexed in excitement.

We are moving to St. Louis. His parents live there and I got accepted to Wash U for fall. I'm so excited!

I was silent. We had grown apart in the last couple of months. She had been a constant in my life until then, sometimes my only support system. Anxious regretful tingles rushed through my core.

Cari hugged Vicky and said, Oh my god girl! I am so happy for you! Congratulations!

Congratulations guys. We'll have to come visit, Frank said.

Yeah, congratulations, I said looking at the floor.

Vicky touched my arm, looked down at me and said, We'll be in touch. Don't worry Dughall.

What's next for you guys? Cari said.

Oh, you know, I'm just waiting for him to propose. We're both short on money right now but he starts a job in June. So maybe sometime shortly after. That's what I'm hoping anyway!

Cari squealed and said, I am so happy for you!

I looked at Brent. He was stoic. Proud. He held her tight as they left. Cari hugged me. Slowly grinding my crotch. I looked at Frank making sure he hadn't seen. He hadn't. He sat in the dining room smoking a cigarette and drinking a beer. We joined him.

Dughall, you should read me some of your poetry, Cari said.

I shot her a glare, embarrassed she would bring

that up. Frank looked up at me.

You write poetry? I didn't know that, he said.

Cari gave me a knowing look and said, He's been writing other stuff too, but he won't show me.

I'd like to read it sometime Dughall.

Uncertain he was truthful I looked over at him. His face was serious.

I really would man. You know I'm minoring in English Lit.

I nodded and said, I know. Maybe I could let you read a few of my poems.

That'd be great.

We made small talk. Talking about college. Our plans afterward. I had forgotten that Frank had such an interest in literature. I squeezed Cari's hand. Her face was proud. She loved me. And I loved her.

Eighteen

Frank called a week later. He wanted to show me his new house. His grandmother had passed away recently and he was her only grandchild. She left him a good amount of money and he had used it for a down payment. He was still unpacking but had managed to display his books on the built-in bookshelves that lined the living room. It looked like a library.

Dughall I read your poetry. It was good. Maybe more alliteration and fewer words.

I waited for more. But he just sat there casually smoking a cigarette. It hadn't hurt as much as I thought it would. I glanced around the room at the shelves.

I didn't know you had so many books, I said.

Yeah. When mom used to teach, another teacher who was retiring gave her several boxes. That's where most of these came from. You're welcome to borrow any of them anytime you want.

I nodded and noted some titles I had intended to read. It was because of this introduction to Frank's library that I began to question college. It had begun to bore me. I liked working on cars so why shouldn't I quit? I could gain mental stimulation through reading. Studying. That's all college was. I returned to Frank's nearly each weekend to get another book and talk to him about literature.

I continued with school through winter and spring

but decided to quit after the spring semester. Cari would graduate in May and her classes became more difficult. We didn't see each other as much. The strain on the relationship grew and we began scheduling mini-dates. Sometimes we would drive to some of my favorite nature areas. During the spring the warm smell and colorful post-thunderstorm sunsets painted trees and grass with the golden pink hue of the skies. At twilight we would dance until the moon illuminated our blue faces. Listening to crickets and frogs and coyotes broke the stress of college and work.

In spring, our connection once again deepened and our honest love stood proud. I found myself looking at rings. I chose a silver band. Prongs holding a diamond.

I planned a picnic on a hill near my grandparents old farm. The hill overlooked the Missouri river bottoms and was one of the best views in the area. On that day, it was humid but only eighty degrees. Making it comfortable to lounge in the sun. Air clear country-crisp we spread out the blanket. Grasshoppers leapt away in waves. We sat hand in hand unpacking lunch. She looked like Judy Garland. Pigtails. Blue checkered sundress. Barefoot and beautiful.

We ate sandwiches. Apples. My breathing was short. Heartbeat fast. I shook and shivered when she looked away to enjoy the view. For a moment I lost myself as I have many times in the nature surrounding us.

Buzzards spiraled above the hills. Hawks cried. Frogs sang. Serene trees. The sweet aroma of river and farm fields filled my nose. I reached in my pocket making sure the ring was there. I held it in my pocket fearful it may fall out. I thought about what to say until I heard myself speak. As if in some distance voice.

Cari, when I met you I knew you were someone special. We had something from that first meeting, a bond that I can't explain. These last six months proved that and have been the greatest of my life. I love you more than I've loved anyone and wanted to share my life with yours. Cari, will you marry me?

The ring sparkled as I held it out. Her hands covered the thousand mile wide smile on her face.

Yes! Of course I will!

We kissed on that blanket under the sun. The trees. Under the blanket of blue. Aware of none of it, only buried in our embrace. There was nothing more important nor engrossing than our love.

Nineteen

After the proposal we began planning the wedding. We went to stores and talked with planners. I called Vicky and told Frank. They were happy for us. I was happy too, but I also recalled the accident. It had been almost a year. Her death gnawed at me. I would drive slow at night. My face hovered close to the windshield scanning the sides of the road. Anyone walking along the road made me want to vomit. In bed, I would sometimes feel the heavy weight of glass on my chest. I didn't tell anyone. Each day seemed to be leading the accident.

Summer came. And mid-July. I almost wished I would die before the date so I wouldn't have to face it. I feared the visions would resurface, but they didn't. On the outside I think everyone thought I was alright. I was doing what I wanted and marrying the girl I loved. What a wonderful life.

The day before the memorial Dmitri called me. He wanted me to come over to the trailer. I felt nervous and didn't know what to expect. Dmitri was usually more brazen. Blunt. Outspoken about why he wanted me to come over. He seemed different. Though I hadn't been smoking much since the accident I smoked on the way over to his place. Dmitri walked out of the trailer. Hat askew. Shirtless. Two beers in his hands and cigarette hanging from his lips.

Here ya go brotha.

He handed me the beer. A twinkle in his eye. We climbed up in the bed of the truck watching the sky change with the sunset. We were silent. It had been three hundred sixty four days since I had drag raced and my life had seemed normal and carefree. It felt so complicated now. As if hearing my thoughts Dmitri shook his head, drinking the rest of the beer. He lit another cigarette.

Ya know Dughall, he said, inhaling then exhaling, This goddam world is misguided.

I nodded. He rarely spoke in this tone. He sounded so serious.

Me and you Dughall, we got this desire to just live the moment, fuck the rest. I known you for five years, seen you have so much fun in cars and this last year you've been broken. Finally had the balls to hook up with my sister but I ain't seen the Dughall I knew. I ain't even seen you drive the shit outta that car.

He waved his hand at the Camaro, cigarette between index and middle finger.

You've gone to school and shit but you ain't happy I can tell. You don't have that spirit anymore. A year ago yer shit got fucked up. Hardcore shit. Some selfish chick thought she could end her life by having somebody else do it for her. She didn't have the balls to do it herself. God rest her soul but damn, what selfishness. I tried to save her, but her eyes already told me she was gone. It wasn't the first time I seen those eyes ya know?

He stopped talking, looking out towards the woods puffing his cigarette. I said nothing. I stared at the side of his face. His eyes moistened before he got up to grab another beer from the trailer. He was right, something was missing. She had taken it. Returning with three more beers, he handed me one. I chugged the remainder of my first and opened the second. He coughed and cleared his throat.

I ever tell you bout my uncle? he said.

Not really, just that he committed suicide ten years ago or so.

Yep. I saw him.

You saw him do it?

He puffed his cigarette and said, Yep. I was eleven years old and was walking to his house from ma and pa's to see if he could come over and help pa move some stuff in the house. I was too weak to help'im. I walked up to the door and just walked in like I always did, we were all family and just as I was shutting the door, I could see my uncle's shadow on the wall of the hall, gun to his head. The same time the door shut, he pulled the trigger. Blasted his brains out. I didn't know what to do so I rushed in to try and help'im. He had a big hole from that .357 on the right side of his head. Blood was everywhere. His eyes were glazed over, looking right at me. I remember closing my eyes and walking away waking up in the hallway a couple minutes later. I ran home and told pa. It was the only time I ever saw him cry.

He lit another cigarette and opened his third beer. We sat on the truck bed. Drinking. Smoking. Staring.

Twenty

After listening to Dmitri that night I began looking at old hot rods again. I bought a 1968 Chevrolet Chevelle. Black paint. Chrome wheels. The engine was stock but I had been piecing one together out of some stuff I had laying around. During winter I became engrossed. Piecing together the perfect engine. Cari was busy with her new job and wedding planning.

We grew apart.

It was unintentional. The wedding was planned for December and felt like something we were supposed to do. Since I had a muscle car again I suggested that we take it to a car show. We met with other motorheads. Hung out with Frank and Dmitri again. It felt good but it wasn't the same as it used to be and I wondered how long it would be until I raced again.

I couldn't get myself to go over seventy on any road. Day or night. What used to be my greatest skill had disappeared. As if this anxiety were not enough, many of my racing friends seemed different. They greeted me as if a simple acquaintance, acknowledging neither my new car nor the accident. Nevertheless, Dmitri, Frank, Cari and I went each Friday and Saturday night to the downtown car show. Frank would drive his Charger. Dmitri, when he wasn't drunk would drive his Trans Am.

One Saturday in August, a tenseness that

reminded me of my accident lurked in the air. We met downtown as usual. Cari and I picked up Dmitri. Drunk. Loud. Wobbly. He immediately wandered off when we got to the car show. It was a sunny day. Air warm, humid. People wore shorts, hats and t-shirts. Some men walked around shirtless, shaved chests and suntanned golden bronze skin. Women walked in bikini tops. Their breasts, perky nipples caused each man and boy to stare.

Frank met us there and we sat in lawn chairs soaking in the sun by the Chevelle and the Charger when a commotion rose nearby. I jumped up. Rushed toward it. I could feel it, Dmitri had done something foolish. I pushed through a crowd of motorheads and beautiful loud cars shining splendid translucent colors. A circle formed around two men. Both shirtless. One broad-shouldered massive belly, shoulder length blonde hair. I knew him as Francis. He drove an ugly late seventies Mustang.

The other was Dmitri. Lean muscled tan skin, tiny beer belly pooching over what would be a six pack above his unbuttoned pants. His shirt in hand. Baseball hat still on crooked sideways like usual. Face red and angry, Francis shouted at him.

Come on mother fucker, you're so fucking bad, come over and hit me!

I don't want to fight you.

You gonna keep after my daughter I'll piss in your mouth, rip off your head then shit down your gullet you fucking asshole.

Darius, a guy I had raced several times walked up beside me.

Damn man, he really pissed Francis off.

Yeah what'd he do?

Aw man, you don't know? Dmitri's been after his sixteen year old daughter, Nancy for a while now, got caught making out with her in Francis' car and now he got caught with the girl's mouth wrapped round his sausage.

I shook my head, Oh fuck.

A pretty blonde haired girl, pigtails bikini top daisy dukes pushed her way through the crowd behind Francis.

Dad, stop! I like him, leave him alone!

Francis seemed to ignore her. He raised his fists, walked toward Dmitri who stood stoic. Arms still down at his sides. His face seemed to smile at the situation. He no longer wobbled. Somehow steady though I knew the alcohol hadn't worn off. He watched Francis advance.

Dad!

Nancy continued screaming. Unable to follow Francis. Her mother and brother holding her. I thought briefly of stepping in to help Dmitri but froze, mesmerized by the inaction and tension. I also knew Dmitri could scrap.

Francis sweaty, short guttural breaths, rushed at Dmitri with hands outstretched as if to strangle him. Dmitri stepped easily aside. In the same motion he extended a fist, catching Francis on the chin. Francis stumbled, falling wildly, landing on his hands and belly. Chuckles rose from the crowd as he stood up. Gravel stuck to his skin. His fists curled tight as he advanced again. This time he slowed his advance. Like a boxer, Dmitri circled, tossing his shirt behind him.

They danced for about ten seconds, then Dmitri launched a punch that missed. As he pulled away Francis tackled him. Dmitri could've stood a chance in the boxing match but now I feared the worst. Francis was nearly three times heavier than Dmitri. Dmitri stood little chance on the ground. I looked over at Nancy. Tears falling. Covering her face in her hands. Lowering herself to the ground. Somebody in the crowd yelled for someone to call the police.

I leaned over to Darius and said, We gotta do something, man.

He chuckled.

Good luck with that.

I jumped in the ring. Butterflies in my stomach. Expecting to be beaten severely.

Alright guys break it up.

Francis looked up like a lion ready to feed and said, What the fuck are you gonna do, you scrawny fuck?

I looked at Dmitri. His face calm telling me to go. A big fist smashed Dmitri's face. It crinkled. Bloody. Swollen. I put a hand on Francis' shoulder. His big arm and shoulder flung me back. Dmitri writhed on the ground trying to escape. Francis raised his fist high and punched Dmitri again and again. Dmitri managed to cover his head, in turn receiving blows to the ribs. Again I stepped in. This time ready to kick Francis in the face.

Francis, get off that man now!

I looked over as Sergeant Hampton emerged from the crowd. Francis looked at him. Fists falling to his side. Dmitri's body was limp. His face resting on the asphalt. Blood slowly pooled.

Goddam bastard was fucking with my little girl!

Francis, I don't care what happened. Get off that kid and put your hands on your head. I gotta take you in.

Francis looked down at Dmitri. Scowling as if he wanted to keep beating him. Cari ran up next to me.

Is it true?

I nodded as she looked at me. Her eyes wet. She walked toward Francis. Her fists clenched. Face red. He stared at her with a smirk. I grabbed her arm.

Cari, c'mon he ain't worth it. He'll get his.

She beat my chest with her fists.

Why didn't you do anything?

Each strike less harsh until they rested limply on my stomach. She buried her face in my chest. Bawling and screaming. Sergeant Hampton cuffed Francis and took him away. A few minutes passed until the EMTs showed up. Slowly turning Dmitri over. His face already purple.

Blood stained. I looked away. Holding Cari's face to my chest so she wouldn't see. The crowd dispersed. Car engines revving. Laughter erupting as if everything was okay. That it had all been a joke. The world seemed to howl in laughter, circling my head like a helicopter reverberating against the concrete walls and black asphalt.

Twenty-One

A day after the fight Cari kept telling me that I should've stopped it. That it was my fault Dmitri was in the hospital. I told her I had tried to stop it. She didn't listen.

Dmitri's hospital stay revealed a high blood-alcohol content, broken jawbone and broken rib. I went to see him nearly every day after work. Sometimes Cari would go. She had a hard time looking at his swollen face. He was always happy to see us. Jawbone wired shut. Waving me in. He could talk but he wrote notes often. In these he revealed his peace with Francis. No retaliation. It was just like him. Forgiveness so easily given after a fight. Whoever won deserved respect. But I knew him too well, the relationship with Nancy wasn't over.

During one visit he wrote on a notepad, Get me the fuck outta here. I need to get some pussy.

I laughed, unsure if he was joking or serious.

Highjack a wheelchair while I unhook this shit and let's ditch this motherfucker.

He reached for the tubes but I held up my hands.

Dude, we can't do that. These people are just trying to help.

He smiled, shrugging like he hadn't been serious.

I need to see her, he said

Who? Cari? Your mom?

Nancy.

I stared at him. His eyes mischievous.

Goddam are you serious? I said.

He nodded his head, flashed a thumbs up, pointed at the first line he had written, Get me the fuck outta here. I need to get some pussy.

Though wounded and vulnerable he remained persuasive. I looked over my shoulder toward the door hoping somehow a nurse hadn't read what he wrote. I shook my head and said, I can't man. You'll be out soon but I don't think I'd mess around with her anymore.

I think I love her, he wrote.

I stared at him, his wired jaw and blue cheeks. Perhaps he could read my emotion as he lowered his head back onto his pillow, leaning back. Obviously a sign it was my time to go. I got up. Angry that he refused to follow Nancy's father's wishes. Driving away I knew something more would come from this situation. The fight was far from over as Dmitri lay in the hospital.

A day after that visit he left the hospital and stayed with his parents for the five weeks it took for him to recover. It was mid-September when he went back to his trailer. He stayed alone more often now. He didn't call me like he used to. I worried about him, so did Cari. She visited him often. Usually finding him drunk in the bed of his truck rambling to himself. I tried to avoid him but at the same time afraid he was mad at me.

One night at the grocery store everything became too much. Fluorescent lights bright as the sun. Packages colorful. I became instantly overwhelmed. The sounds too. Intercom. Children. Early night drunks talking loudly in the aisles. At the register my awareness of self was so magnified I looked at the cashier. So beautiful. She understood each of my thoughts. My eyes looked away from hers. Blushing. Staring at the floor. They flitted. One tile to another. Ignoring detail my body reacted to her automatically. I handed her cash when she asked. Answered fine at her formal query. My breath short. Chest pounding. I left. I wanted to puke.

My thoughts carried a melancholy introspective resonance. I got home finding Cari had left to go check on Dmitri. I collapsed on the bed, waking in the morning as she was getting ready for work. I told her I didn't feel like going to work and was going to call in. After she left I called work. My boss didn't seem to care.

Around noon I threw a notebook in my car and left, drove the Chevelle to a solitary lake. It was a fresh Midwest day. Everything lush. Not too humid or hot. Sun high in the sky. The gravel road was dry and bumpy. Dust erupted from my tires like fog from a freezer. I pulled off. Parked on the grass, walked to the pond with the notebook in my hand. A fallen tree hovered over the pond. I shimmied up so I sat looking out across the water and forest and field. I felt like a child again.

I took out the notebook and began to write. It was the first time I lost myself in the words, motion and thoughts. The occupation became spiritual. Hands. Body. Mind. Synonymous. Gathering the experience. Words. Time. Into one glorious expression. Such is writing. At times arduous and boring. Others fruitful. The next morning I read what I wrote.

> Sometimes the wonder of the earth and normalcy of the familiar make me want to wander away into the night. Just drive. The cold air mixes with the heater flushing my cheeks. As I drive I imagine dark magic creeks flowing away from everything leaving civilization buried in its own diseased filthy degrading existence. A perfection exists here by these creeks. And it's so simple.
>
> They are only creeks. Not rivers or lakes or ponds. Flowing with urine and oil and feces. Crying down hills into the nature, its joy forever lost to childhood innocence for everything true that we see now will be destroyed and buried and lost. And my wonder replaced by wandering takes me nowhere but back to nothing. Back to the melancholy of life.

Twenty-Two

In early October, to reconnect, Cari and I planned a trip to the beach in Corpus Christi, TX. We needed to be alone together and bond and share life. We woke early in the morning and drove the fifteen hours. Too tired to go to the beach we crashed on plush hotel pillows. The next day we made love, staying in bed until noon. That evening we went to the ocean. Feeling the peace. The humid salty air. Seagulls screeching as I sat topless on sand looking out at the ocean. I was glad to share it with Cari.

Seagulls played in the air. The sea whispered tales of fishermen and adventurers who died living. Living just as we were. We said nothing as the sea spoke as it had spoken to billions before. Our hands grasped gently intertwined fingers caressing, speaking, spilling our hearts without words.

Do you think people will do this a hundred years from now? Cari asked.

I hope.

I glanced away. Across the beach. She nodded, probably lost in thought. Perhaps pondering when an ancient message bottle would brush her toe or when a dolphin would jump out of the water or when I would kiss her. I thought about these things too. But it seemed there was something greater, something more than human happening now. Maybe it was god. I don't know. I don't know if she or he even existed. Maybe it's just nature.

The stare across the waves became a trance. Cari watched the waves too, her eyes reflecting the sunset's gleam. I could see her soul, beautiful luminescent radiating like the sun. This was that moment when life stands still. Everything is as perfect as it will ever be. I stare at her as she watches the sun set over the city. The longest most wonderful sunset of my life.

Cari reached over, took my arm and leaned into me. Our shadows swallowed in the faint pink glimmer of sunlight fading away into the west. The waves rhythm thumping like it does forever. And there under the moon something powerful happened. A revelation. Love and nature are all that has ever existed and all anyone needs, I thought. I nod and smile and say nothing as Cari lays her head on my lap and looks up at the stars. I close my eyes and dream that it could all end like this. Beautiful euphoric glorious rhythmic night of discovery.

We were tourists for that week. We walked. Our pale skin on the white sidewalks. Everyone stared at us. We enjoyed each other's company. We rode horses on the beach. Watched water sweeping gently up the sand. We laughed. Spoke seriously. But the week ended quickly. We drove home. Stressed upon leaving leisure behind. Reentering life with its dramatic, monotonous civilization of highways and interstates and large cities. Once on the road our nerves were on edge. The uncomfortable feeling I had grown to only understand as annoyance grew with each mile finally exploding upon arriving in Dallas.

Where do I turn?! I said, staring at all the concrete circling around us.

It should be up here. Quit yelling at me.

I need to know where we are supposed to go before we get there!

We won't get lost! We have a map and we can just turn around if we do! It's not a big deal!

I increased the speed of the car, my hands tight on the wheel and a headache on my temples. She screamed at me stop and I realized my mistake. Emotional, tired and feeling a strange sensation of sadness I pulled over onto the shoulder. Silent.

What are you doing?! she said.

I tilted my head forward. I wanted to sleep. I wanted to make everything okay. I wanted everything to be simple. The only sound was the heavy whoosh of cars and trucks passing us. I felt her hand rub my head.

What's wrong?

I don't know.

We said nothing more. I did not understand what had happened. I knew I was tired. Sad. I wanted to lay down on a bed in a dark room and sleep it all away. She was concerned. Her brow furrowed. But I didn't know how tell her. If I didn't understand, how could she?

Twenty-Three

We got back in town late that night. Cari drove the rest of the way and I slept. In the morning she went to Dmitri's. She called me when she got there. Her voice frantic, more frantic than I'd heard before.

Dughall get over here!

I hadn't talked to Dmitri in a couple weeks. He had been a shell of the man I had known. I feared the worst, that he was laying face down in the grass amid his vomit or his head busted open after tripping in a drunken state. I jumped in the Chevelle, roasting the tires as I took off. I forgot about nearly every anxiety on the trip but it slightly occurred to me as I hit ninety. I didn't care, I just wanted to help my friend.

When I got to the trailer, Dmitri was wobbling and yelling at Cari. Nancy sat on the tailgate of Dmitri's truck. Tight shirt. No bra. I pulled into the drive. Dmitri simply glanced at me. Unexcited. Unconcerned. I shut off the car and slowly got out.

Dmitri! What's going on?!

Just fuck off man! Mind yer damn bizness.

I looked over at Nancy, her face emotionless. Eyes avoiding mine. Cari was crying. She came over to lean on my shoulder. It was implied that my job was to sober him up. Talk sense into him. I also knew we needed to get Nancy out of here. This was not the place for her. I looked down at the top of Cari's head.

Cari can you go make some coffee? I said.

She looked up at me, makeup streaking down her cheeks eyes moist. She nodded. Emotions high, she was still gorgeous. I gently kissed her lips before she walked into the trailer. Dmitri cracked open another beer and began to drink it as I walked toward him.

I don't think you need another beer, man.

Fuck you.

Come on Dmitri, will you at least sit down?

I motioned to the bed of his truck where Nancy still sat. She looked at the ground. He shook his head, stumbling away from me nearly tripping on a fallen branch. I let him go. Looking toward the Chevelle, I felt uneasy. While Dmitri peed on the dead leaves, Nancy looked up at the road where a loud vehicle crunched gravel. Exhaust echoed against the trees. I clenched my fists as the truck slid to a stop blocking Dmitri's driveway.

Francis jumped out, red faced. Truck still running, door open, fists balled up. Nancy's twin brother Stan followed holding a rifle.

Goddammit! I have to kill you all? said Francis.

I stood frozen, unsure where to go. Wondering if they could see Dmitri or if Cari knew what was going on. Francis motioned to Nancy, his belly quivering underneath his yellow shirt.

Get the fuck over here girl! How many times have

I told you to stay away from these bastards?!

But Dad, I like him, Nancy said.

Girl you get over here now. We don't like these goddam, know it all mother-fuckers.

Francis, I said.

Shut the fuck up boy. I wish I'd had the chance to smash your face in that fight too. Now I guess I just gotta rip your head off.

I felt a wetness on my neck then and knew I'd been shot somehow. I did not feel afraid any longer. I only wanted to charge Francis. Give him all I had left. I nearly did until I saw the beer can hurtling over my head toward Francis, sprinkling the earth. The can landed a good distance to the left of Francis. Certainly farther than Dmitri had intended. I touched the wet spot. It wasn't red. I touched it to my lips. Beer.

Fuck off, fatty, Dmitri said in slurred speech behind me.

You want me to break the rest of the bones in your body you worthless fuck? Francis said, slowly advancing toward us.

Bring it on, motherfucker.

I glanced behind me. Dmitri's eyes barely able to focus. Body wobbling. One punch would do him in. I took a breath. The last time I had been forced into a fight was a couple years ago with Dmitri. There had been four of them. Dmitri took out two but I only managed one. I took him out from sheer adrenaline. The second had proved to be the better fighter and had broken my nose. I knew this would be much worse.

How about I just fucking shoot you both, leaving you for the possums and vultures? That's all you're good for, you worthless motorheads, Francis said, gesturing at the rifle in Stan's hands.

I suggest a fair fight, I said.

You saw what I did to your fucking buddy behind you, you want me to send you to the hospital too?

I shrugged, looking over my shoulder at Dmitri who appeared oblivious. Francis walked toward me.

Stop right there Francis! Cari said and stepped out of the trailer with Dmitri's pistol in her hand.

What the fuck are you gonna do darling?

Cari moved her hand slightly, firing a shot into the bed of Francis's truck.

I already called the Sheriff. So I'd suggest leaving. You just saw how good a shot I am.

Alright missy, we'll leave, but this shit ain't over.

Francis chuckled and waved Stan and Nancy toward the truck.

But dad . . . Nancy said.

Francis grabbed her arm and shoved her in the truck. He started to walk to the driver's side and I said, Francis, how bout you drop the whole thing if I beat you in a race tonight?

He stopped and looked at my Chevelle and said, How fast is this thing?

Dunno, I haven't taken it to the track.

A large grin crossed his face.

I'll run you. What the hell. Meet at nine on Old Highway 94 at the quarry.

He retained his smile as he walked to his truck. Just before opening the door he turned and said, You're going down, boy.

He got in the truck and peeled out. Swinging the bed sideways. Tires belched dirt and he was gone. I turned to Cari.

Where's the Sheriff? He should be here by now.

I bluffed, she said and shrugged, I half-hoped he would charge one of you. I was ready to shoot him.

Gun lowered at her side she stood looking at Dmitri. He wobbled.

Do you think you can beat him?

I don't know. His Mustang's ugly but it could be fast. I've never seen him race. One thing is for sure, I need to tweak the Chevelle. It's gotta be faster.

Twenty-Four

Evening came quick. My heartbeat echoed in my head. Stomach jostled to the beat. I hustled to put a nitrous system on the Chevelle. I had never used nitrous before. It had come from Dmitri, something he had always intended to use on the Trans Am but never did. It was a one hundred fifty horsepower shot. I hoped it wouldn't blow the motor. I got it all set up by seven, enough time for a couple passes on the asphalt just up the road. I worried about everything that could go wrong. Engine could blow. The Chevelle would be too slow. I would lose.

But Cari told me not to worry and said, You'll be fine. You were a good driver and that doesn't just disappear. I knew she was just as worried as I was though. She tried to relax Dmitri. Bring him down from his drunkenness. About seven thirty he fell asleep. Cari told me she wanted to stay with him to make sure he didn't do anything stupid. I agreed.

I left and grabbed a cheap burger from Burger Stand. Stomach twirled. I headed toward old Highway 94. I estimated the Chevelle would be running slightly faster than the Nova with the nitrous but not by much. Hopefully it would be enough. I wondered about Francis, how fast was the Mustang? I wished Cari or Dmitri were here like the old days before Jessica Hall, before Nancy, when we were just kids having fun. I wondered where it all went wrong.

The accident. The goddam accident. I prepared myself to drive over the spot where I hit her. I imagined her now walking in front of the car with her arms outstretched. My stomach sank, nearly vomiting up the burger. I slowed down, fifteen under the limit as I passed the white cross and flowers on the left side of the road. I don't know why but I saluted as if she were some soldier, dying in battle to save mankind. I took a deep breath, hoping to slow my anxious heart. I was in no shape to race. I wondered if Francis had done this on purpose.

As I pulled into the quarry's wide drive, Francis and his son stood in front of a 1970 Dodge Dart. Boxy body. Wide eyed headlights. Hood scoop. His smile told me he had indeed set up this spot on purpose. We would likely end where I had raced the Nova for the last time. Adding to this was that I had never seen this car before.

How bout we run a quarter that way? Francis said, pointing in the direction of the accident.

I shrugged, trying to act cool. But nervousness overtook me. I was shaking, hoping he wouldn't want to shake hands. Behind me I heard another Dodge engine purr. At first I was even more nervous until I realized I knew the sound of the exhaust. Turning around I saw Frank get out of his Charger.

He waved and said, Hey Dughall. Cari called me and thought you could use some backup.

He glanced at Francis. Francis' face dropped slightly but the clever smile returned. He laughed and said, Two worthless motorheads. Doesn't matter, you're still going down.

Frank's cool demeanor calmed me as he lit a cigarette and waved his hand at the Dart and said, What do you have in that thing anyway? I've never seen it around.

You'll find out.

Without hesitation, as if anticipating this response, Frank walked over to the Dart, reached into the grill and popped the hood. I followed. Francis laughed.

It's just a 360. Nothing special.

The engine bay was a clean aluminum mass staring back at me. The carburetor rose high on the intake manifold. The large valve covers shone. Frank took a drag from his cigarette.

Looks like a 440 to me. Let's hear it.

Francis stared at Frank a moment, eyes flaring. He had hoped this all to be a surprise. He hadn't expected Frank to show. I was glad he was here. Frank was the most level-headed guy I knew. I had seen many guys try to fight him but he would stare at them as if he didn't care if they killed him or walked away. His stare had the same effect on Francis.

Francis turned the key. I heard the whine of the fuel pump then as the starter kicking out spinning the flywheel, the engine belched to life a slow repetitive bumpity-bumpity thumpthump. Frank turned to me, concerned look on his face as Francis shut it off.

Sounds healthy, said Frank.

Francis smiled, staring at me as he spoke.

Yeah. You should be able to handle it right Dughall? You just have a 406 right?

I nodded.

Let's go then!

Frank touched my shoulder nudging me back to my car.

How fast is the Chevelle compared to the Nova?

I knew he would judge me if I told him the truth, but I did it anyway and said, I don't really know. I've never taken it to the track. The only time I stomped it all the way to the floor was this afternoon outside of Dmitri's place.

He stared at the ground.

I put a hundred fifty shot of nitrous on it today.

He looked up and said, You never use nitrous.

I know, but Dmitri's life may depend on this race.

He reached up again and patted my back.

Alright man, I've got your back if anything goes wrong. Go balls out, don't think, just race. You've got this.

I nodded, climbing into the Chevelle. Frank walked out toward the road ready to flag the race after we did our burnouts.

Alright baby, we've got to give this race our all, I said to the car as I bumped the ignition. The car thumped and rumbled as I pulled into the road. Francis followed. My lights shone on the cornfields, glowing in golden beige. The blue half-moon above seemed to twinkle as I glanced up. I took a deep breath. Cool moist river smell. Sweet mist of corn filled my lungs. Nerves calm now as I breathed. Hands steady as I pulled the car into position.

Twenty-Five

As Francis stalled the engine to around 4,000 RPM I looked over. He was grinning, staring straight ahead, gripping steering wheel, hand wrapped around the shifter. The Dart sounded damn good. The Chevelle roared as I followed Francis' lead, pushing the pedal to match the transmission speed. I prepared to launch out fast. Under the moonlight, Frank looked like a ghost. His hands raised high. It made me shiver in memory of her.

As Frank's arms fell, my foot came off the brake. The Chevelle lurched forward in a twisted launch. Front tires rose slightly off the ground. I felt confident and pulled ahead half a car length. I heard the Dart's exhaust pipes growling hollow grunts. Its headlights surreal against the gray pavement. The Dart's front fender crept past the front of the Chevelle as I heard his RPMs rise. He lurched ahead. I pushed the button. Nitrous injecting oxygen, cooling the intake manifold. I thrust forward nearly even with the Dart. The cars struggled. The Chevelle pulled slightly ahead as we flew over the white spray-painted finish line.

It was then when relief drained that I was aware the speed I was going. My eyes scanned the side of the road for anything, any movement. Francis had sped past, his tail lights far ahead. I was alone and glad I won, yet I also worried that something more waited as I prepared to turn around. I pushed hard on the brakes as I passed the cross and flowers to my right. Her face appeared in the sky. Eyes flaming blue judging my soul. I skidded to a stop, tires squealing, their smoke puffed past the window as a gust of wind blew behind me. The face laughed, disappearing into the stars and a bright light shone through my windshield. My chest felt full of cigarette smoke crushing my organs. The roar of the Dart grew louder, calming me slightly. Francis slid to a stop, smiling.

Looks like you won kid.

I nodded. His face dropped. Smile drooping into a somber twisted expression.

You know this ain't over. Nobody fucks my daughter without my blessing, specially not that bastard!

You said . . .

I didn't say shit kid. Just said I would race you.

And he took off, the Dart's engine screamed. His tires slid across pavement and rocks. Bits of rubber sprinkled the Chevelle. What would I tell Cari? She would hate me. Dmitri needed to forget about Nancy. But I knew he wouldn't. I turned around and drove toward Frank.

Nearing the quarry driveway, dust flew up. Francis and his son peeled out onto the road swinging the back end of the car into the other lane. His taillights became red dots against the fields. I drove into the dust cloud. Frank sat in his car, windows up surrounded by a swirling tan mist. I pulled next to him, the dust blowing away. He rolled his window down. His body jerking to the rhythm of his car's engine.

Francis said you won.

Yeah I beat him. But I don't know . . .

Whatta ya mean? You won . . .

I don't know if this is over Frank.

Frank shook his head and said, There isn't much we can do right now. Want to go grab a brew before we head back to the trailer?

Sure, Patty's is on the way.

Twenty-Six

Frank and I drove to Patty's but I felt uneasy as we raised our glasses in a cheers for the race. We listened to the sharp trills coming from the bagpipes and fiddles and voices of the band on stage. Cigarette smoke curled from our mouths. Drunken shouts rose throughout the bar. It would've been a great experience had I not been worried about Cari and Dmitri.

Do you think they're okay?

Frank looked at me awkwardly and said, What do you mean?

I don't know exactly but I feel like something will happen. Maybe I'm just paranoid.

Frank cocked his head sideways and shrugged.

The song Rocky Road to Dublin rose from the stage and a joyful cheer, clinking glasses came from all around us. It was hard not to be happy and carefree in an Irish pub. I raised my glass and chugged the rest.

Frank lit a cigarette and said, What do you want to do? Do you think we should go?

Yeah. You wanna follow me or what?

Yeah I'll follow you.

We paid the tab and left. Our cars seemed silent as their engines cranked over. I felt frightened and anxious as if the world were changing. The breeze wafted the sounds of frogs and grasshoppers into my ears. I drove fast on the dark midnight highway. Trees cast vague creepy shadows across fields. The tree-line wooded roadways harbored every nightmarish childhood monster. Frank's Charger struggled to keep pace on the moonlit gray blue straightaways. His round headlights faded as the Chevelle propelled forward in a hard tug. Its headlights showing insects like dust in a projector. Nearing the turn for Dmitri's trailer the air became silent and heavy. There were no sounds but the cars.

And then I heard a series of gunshots followed by a solitary shot. I pulled off the pavement onto the dirt drive. Frank followed. My headlights shone at the scene. Francis' truck was crunched against the front end of Dmitri's Trans Am. My stomach instantly grew nauseous. Flipping. Tumbling. Aware something terrifying waited beyond this.

Frank rushed up behind me and said, I'm calling the police.

I nodded and said, I'm going to check the trailer.

Frank pulled out his cell phone and dialed as I walked toward the trailer. I left my headlights on so I could see easier. As I neared I could see a large man on the porch, shouting words I could not understand. Another voice came from within the trailer. It sounded like Cari's. High-pitched shrill. The way it sounded when she was stressed. Then there were two more gunshots. The large man collapsed on the porch. I ran toward the trailer.

As I ran I saw a body. It lay feet first, one leg bent folding over the other. A beer bottle lay next to it. Foam still bubbling on the dead brown red leaves. The man's t-shirt was pulled up a little above his belly button. The t-shirt was off-white. The chest of the shirt where once there was a design or writing was ripped with several small diameter holes. They were soaked in dark red. The face of the man at first appeared serene. The downhill angle of the body did not allow for me to see it immediately. But I knew it was Dmitri. His baseball hat cocked sideways still on his head. As I walked closer I could see his eyes. A still smoking cigarette lay on the ground next to his mouth.

His eyes reminded me how he had described his uncle's. Cold. Glassy. Lifeless. The holes in his chest bleeding. He did not move. I nearly passed out but knew I had to check on Cari. I could do nothing for Dmitri now. I had heard no other sound coming from the trailer and walked cautiously toward it. Francis lay on the porch. He was breathing heavily and looked up at me with wide eyes. There were two bullet holes in his chest. Blood was soaking his shirt. A gun lay next to his hand. He did not reach for it and he did not speak. I called out for Cari.

Dughall? she said.

The kitchen light turned on and Cari walked into the empty doorway. She held Dmitri's revolver in her hands and looked down at Francis. His eyes were glassy now. Her face quivered. She dropped the gun and rushed toward me. I held her there for a moment, just letting her cry and shake.

What happened? I said.

It took her a moment to clear the sobs from her throat and then she said, I think he killed Dmitri. I woke up to a crash and Dmitri told me to stay inside. He went and checked on it and then I heard gunshots and yelling. Then it was quiet. I went in Dmitri's room and got his gun. And . . . god . . . Dughall that's when the door opened. And I said something and heard Francis say he would kill me too. He held a gun at his waist and was smiling. He stared at me for a minute and then started to raise the gun and walk toward me. That's when I . . . I shot him.

Tears streaked her face. I nodded and looked over her shoulder as we embraced. I said nothing but held her close. Frank walked up beside us. His face somber. He nodded at me and lit a cigarette as he looked at the porch.

It didn't take long for the medics and sheriff's deputies to get there. Casting blue red flashing lights on the cars and trucks and forest. It lent soft sober realization to the scene. Each of us knowing no more violence would rise from the situation. They talked to each of us separately and took Cari back to the station for questioning.

Cari's parents had arrived shortly before the deputies took her. I told them what had happened. The sorrow of parents losing a child echoed throughout the countryside. Frank chain-smoked almost an entire pack of cigarettes but otherwise showed no emotion. Cari's parents told me to go home and get some rest while they went with Cari. I stood there staring into the woods trying to believe that this was all a dream. The area was taped off and we were told it was time for us to go.

Frank nudged me and said, Dude you okay?

Yeah I'm alright.

He nodded. His eyes looked tired, his face sagged.

I'm gonna go home but I can hang with you if you want, he said.

I'll be fine. I'm going home too.

Alright. If you need anything call me okay?

Okay.

He pulled me close for a hug then took a flask from his pocket. He looked at it a moment before handing it to me. It was Dmitri's. The top and bottom were silver with a large band of black leather wrapped around the middle. On the front, a black sticker with white letters read Fuck.

I grabbed this for you. Thought you might want it.

I smiled sadly as I took it and said, Thanks.

We walked back to our cars. My shoulders heavy. Head foggy as I started the car. It was nearly four in the morning. I did not feel tired. The drive back to the apartment was filled with memories of the last six years. I pulled into the parking lot. The air soft as the last hour before dawn usually was. The Chevelle's exhaust melted away the peaceful air. I parked and shut it off. I sat in the dim parking lot and leaned back my seat.

I woke to a kid knocking on my window.

Mister are you okay? Mister?

I sat up, sun flashing off the chrome mirror into my eye. The kid was short and could barely see in my car. His sandy hair, freckled forehead were all I saw.

Yeah kid I'm alright.

Okay. This car is cool.

Thanks.

I couldn't even grin. Thoughts swirled of yesterday's events. I looked over at the passenger seat where I had put the flask. It lay. Fatherless. Lost to the world. I picked it up and sloshed it around. There was still a good amount of liquor in it. I took a sip.

Fuck.

Twenty-Seven

Picking Cari up from her parents' house was sobering. We said nothing as we drove to my apartment. I didn't dare talk about the race or last night or any of it. She didn't either, I suppose. Her face haggard and weary, eyes cold foggy voids. Her parents had said little when I arrived. Mother wept. Father stoic, stared at the floor. I was uneasy. Dmitri was gone. Dead. All over a young girl. I had seen him, eyes open, blood soaked skin. Cari had shot and killed Francis. All for what?

What a stupid damn world.

A few days later, we went to the funeral. Sad grey day. Dmitri's stories were the only smiles. I stood with Cari and her parents. She leaned against me, her eyes too swollen to cry.

It's my fault. It's all my fault, she said.

No. It's not your fault at all, I said.

We repeated this conversation throughout that day and in the days to come. At my apartment, Cari sat on the couch watching cartoons. She appeared emotionless. Eyes dark circles. Face taut. I tried to get her to eat but she insisted on only toast and water. She refused to leave the apartment except to see her mother and father. Each time I tried to talk to her she only squeezed my hand and looked at me with the saddest eyes in the world. Two weeks after the shooting she looked up at me from her seat on the couch.

Dughall, I think I need help.

What do you want to do?

I think I may need to live with my parents for a while until I feel better.

I nodded and said, Is there anything I can do?

She smiled a weak thin smile and reached out to my hand, pressing it between hers. They were thin, cold.

Just be there, she said and squeezed my hand. Her face looked ten years older and thinner than normal. The color in her cheeks and lips was gone. I sat down on the couch and hugged her. We packed her things in silence. There was nothing more to say. I drove her to her parents and felt like a mother who knew her child was dying, taking them one last time to the doctor to confirm the terminal disease. I wanted to believe that she would heal and she would return to me loving me like she used to. But I feared she wouldn't.

She stared straight ahead as I drove. We sat in her parents' drive for a moment knowing this was some sort of goodbye. We would move on from here and hopefully rise from this tragedy together, leaving us able to handle life by embracing it and not submersed in it. I longed for the optimism of love. It still survived somewhere in all this. I stared at the trees. The cedar looked like fur waiting to embrace me. Engulf my sorrow.

I leaned over. Kissed her cheek. She looked at me.

Pitiful eyes saying she wished she could forget all this happened and go back to what we had. Her face told me that this was it. She reached up stroking my face, head slightly cocked, a short smile on her narrow tired face. I moved my mouth to one side, closed mouth, melancholy smile. The goodbye smile of lovers.

Her mother walked outside in the solemn walk of a parent who has lost a child. I climbed out and helped Cari get up and go in the house. Her mother stood on the other side of Cari. None of us spoke. Before we entered the house Cari stopped.

I love you both, she said.

She pulled us toward her allowing the most pure, loving embrace man knows. I wondered what more lay ahead of us as we stood on the concrete surrounded by plants, country air wafting into my nostrils. I sat her down on the couch, unpacked the car and drove away on winding back-roads, gravel puking underneath my tires, passing fields Dmitri and I had driven on dark roadless nights drunk on life. The excitement of discovery and unknown future never a thought. My weary eyes stung but I drove on, past the restaurant where Cari worked in high school, remembering her gorgeous face then and wanting to marry her someday. Gravel dust rose rounding the corner to the trailer. Yellow tape still tied to trees. Dmitri's truck sat sad, lonely.

I got out of the Chevelle and sat in the bed of the

truck wishing I had a beer and a friend like every memorable night spent drinking smoking talking in this same spot watching Dmitri tell stories that may or may not have been true. Sometimes I would listen, hoping he would fall asleep so Cari and I could mess around but mostly I enjoyed his tall tales. His voice. Ideas and actions. I leaned my head against the cab and fell asleep.

Twenty-Eight

I talked to Cari on the phone every day, never for long. The next couple weeks were strange without her around. I felt alone. When I would visit her at her parents' house, I felt even more alone. She was often tired or irritable and time with her wasn't like it used to be.

I had requested vacation a week after the shooting. And just before I left, Cari's parents called to tell me that they were taking her to the hospital to stay until she could care for herself. Even though she had been going to therapy and had received medication, she still refused to eat, experienced insomnia, was increasingly belligerent and irritable and did not seem to care if she lived or died.

I met them at their house on a sunny Monday in October. It smelled like fall outside, musty sweet smell. I had seen her two days before and even in those two days she looked more thin and more pale. Her father and I held each of her arms and carried her to the car.

She kept saying, I don't want to go. Just let me die. Just let me die.

Her mother did not say anything, only looked at the ground.

Her father said, We love you and we're not going to give up on you.

And Cari was silent. She said nothing more after

110

that. I sat in the back with her and held her hand. It was quiet as we drove from the gravel roads to pavement and highways. The sunlight warmed the car. Cari closed her eyes and lay her head on my shoulder. The grass was still green and trees still held yellows and oranges. The behavioral health annex of the hospital sat next to a large green lawn and tree lined street and looked more like a school than a hospital. We parked and Cari looked up. She was wringing her hands. I reached down and gently squeezed them.

She glanced over at me and I smiled and said, I love you.

I love you too.

Her mother went inside and came out with a wheelchair and a nurse. The nurse helped me get Cari into the chair as her parents went inside to fill out paperwork. I stood behind her, hands on her shoulders. When the paperwork was finished they took us to her room. It was small. One bed. A chair. A window. We stayed and talked to the nurse and to Cari for a short time but Cari was tired and dozed off. It was good to see her sleep.

I kissed Cari on the head and we left. Her parents took me to lunch and we talked about work and Frank and Vicky. We did not talk about Dmitri or Cari. But I found myself worrying about Cari. I knew this was the best thing for her now but what would happen to our relationship, I wondered. My hands began to tremble and I felt a tightness in my chest. I wanted to go home.

You ready Dughall? said Cari's father.

Yeah. Yeah I'm ready.

He patted me on the back and we walked to the car. We drove back to their house and I told them goodbye and they said the same. I walked to my car and sat there for a few minutes before leaving. On the way home I drove slowly, afraid Jessica Hall would return to jump in front of my car. And I thought of Dmitri laying on his back. His eyes cold and empty. I went inside but it felt lonely. Quiet. I called Vicky.

Hello? she said.

Hey Vicky, it's Dughall how are you?

I'm doing really good. How are you? How's Cari?

She's not good. Took her to a mental health place today. I guess that's good. I'm . . . I'm not doing too well either I guess. I've been thinking about everything. My parents, Jessica, Dmitri, Cari . . . it's been a lot to happen. I don't know really why I called. Maybe shouldn't have. I'm just a downer.

Dughall . . . you're not a downer. It's just a lot. I really think you should talk to someone.

I've been thinking about it. But I don't know. I never had much luck with that.

You could start jogging or exercising or camping or something. Brent's really into hiking and jogging. Maybe you could try that.

Maybe. I don't know. How is Brent?

We talked about him and college for a while but I kept thinking about camping. My parents and I had gone camping a lot. Maybe it would be good to go again. After I hung up with Vicky I wrote a couple poems and went to the storage locker where the rest of my parents' things were. I found the tote of camping supplies and my dad's old backpack and took it all home.

Twenty-Nine

After reading a book about backpacking and going through all my parents camping supplies I bought some more gear and dried food. The weather in Missouri was warm for October. I thought I could get in a good backpacking trip in the Ozark Mountains. My vacation began and I left the apartment under sunny skies. It was supposed to be in the mid-fifties during the day and forties at night. It should be a good trip.

It felt good to be on the open road. It was a five hour drive to the trailhead and I stopped at a diner for lunch around Ridgedale. It was an old fifties diner. Lead paint peeled off the facade like birch bark. I thought about some kid picking it up and munching on it, remembering it years later and blaming their parents for allowing them to eat paint chips. I chuckled.

I still had a smile on my face when I walked through the door. An old lady at the counter scowled at me. Another middle aged woman looked up as she finished a conversation with a heavyset bearded guy sitting in one of the booths by the window. She smiled, walking toward me.

Hey hon, where would you like to sit?

I shrugged.

Just wherever.

Okay. We can put you over here, hon.

I followed her to a booth. The plastic material on the seat had ripped and had been taped over with packing tape that was now crusty, yellow.

What can I get for ya?

I'll do a coffee, three eggs, toast and bacon.

She nodded, leaving with a smile. I looked around. The walls had pictures of old gas stations, diners and a large neon clock in the middle of the grill area. All the booth seats were light blue plastic covered, many of them ripped like the one I sat on. The cash register was yellow plastic, probably from the early eighties. It smelled like a normal diner, fried eggs, coffee and stale cigarettes. I noted the no smoking sticker on the front door as the bearded man's cigarette smoke curled up onto the grimy ceiling that looked like oil could drip onto me at any moment.

I was hungrier than I thought and finished my food as soon as it arrived. I picked up the bill, left two dollars on the table and went to the register to pay the rest. The old lady glanced over at me, then quickly away making me wonder if there was something wrong with me. After another minute she turned and walked up slowly to the register. Her back arched, fingers bony and crooked. She didn't say anything as she pecked at the keys.

Four twenty five.

I handed her five bucks telling her to keep the change. She scowled again, slamming the register drawer closed and turning her back on me. I shrugged and walked out trying not to dwell on it but I did. The entire drive into the mountains to the trailhead I scowled back at her wishing I would have gone back and said something to her. Told her what I was thinking.

The trailhead parking lot had cars in it and I debated even continuing. I didn't want people to be here. But I grabbed my pack, checked my food and water situation and started walking. I followed the trail until I arrived at a lake and found a clear spot. I set up my tarp tent and started a fire.

Shelter up, fire going, I pulled out some jerky and trail mix. The sun began to set. Pink purple yellow colors floated above the lake. It was worth it to get away like this. I remember how my father talked about going backpacking when he was my age. I wished he were here now. This was far too marvelous. This was worth living. The fire crackled. Wind whispered.

I knew I belonged and that the place I had been searching for was here. Was really everywhere, I just hadn't gone deep enough. The night grew colder and I unrolled the sleeping bag and put on my long sleeve shirt. I lay next to the fire staring at the clear sky. Stars I had never seen. They reminded me of someone I thought I knew until I looked at them closely, realizing they looked completely different than I first thought. I lay under chilly sky. Fire smoldering. I felt alive.

Thirty

The next morning I felt the world changing. Silence. Solitude. Squirrels, rabbits, deer. They spoke to me like a profound novel. One that leaves you breathless that someone wrote it. So profound that you think they mirror your thoughts. As I rolled my bag and folded my tarp I looked out across the lake knowing I would likely never see it again.

Walking through the tree canopy reminded me of childhood. Fishing with my father. Running through my grandfather's fields on his farm. It was perhaps the clearest most lucid day I've had since I was a child. It felt comfortable. Glorious even. My pack somehow comforting on my shoulders, I walked pretty far that day and set up camp amidst a grove of large trees.

I slept restlessly that night. My feet throbbing. I worried about blisters. It had been something I had not considered. And this led to awareness of each noise. Anxiety found me even here. I thought of Cari and Jessica and Dmitri. I wished I could share this with them. I looked up at the stars. The never ending layers of light lent peace and finally around two in the morning I fell asleep.

Three hours later I woke to a shuffling crash. Peeking out of the tarp tent a black bear was tearing apart my backpack. I cringed as I watched it. I was frozen. I imagined myself rushing out to scare it away, stabbing it in the chest multiple times and its body falling limp, eyes staring skyward. My breathing heavy and animalistic. Instead I watched like it were an act in a play. I knew I had to try to stop it. Get it away from the food and my camp. I began rustling my sleeping bag, keeping a pocketknife ready but knowing it would really do nothing. I sang She'll be coming round the mountain . . . in hopes it was enough to startle it. The bear jumped back and stared in my direction as I rose from the tent holding my jacket over my head making me look eight feet tall. It ran away but even in dawn's light I saw food wrappers strewn and dried food scattered in the dirt.

As the sun rose, I began picking up the trash. I realized there was very little salvageable food. It was something I realized I had neglected after I left the car. I was able to save a granola bar and one unopened dehydrated packet of red beans and rice. The rest, roughly a measly days' worth of food was scattered. Mixed with dried pine needles and dirt. My pack was shredded too, making me wonder how I could ever go on or even get back. Everything had fallen apart so quickly. Forced to find a way to keep going I sat trembling, shaking. I reached over and picked up Dmitri's flask and took a swig.

For a couple hours I just sat. Wondering what to do. Give up and leave or leave the mess for the animals or clean it up. I knew I must ration my food now. Overtaken by anxiety I grabbed all the litter, possessions that I could. Hopeful that something more could be salvaged. Though frantic, my actions helped my mind ease. Allowing me to think of alternatives. I was halfway finished with the trail loop, farther than I knew I could travel today and tomorrow. I should have prepared myself for this. My feet hurt and I had barely enough food to last the rest of the day. I decided to let my feet rest for the day and stay here.

I was hungrier than normal and wasn't used to hiking. My father had shown me how to hunt and some survival skills when I was younger and I remembered the way he had made snares. I found a long thin piece of cord which I decided to use. The idea of killing an animal did not appeal to me but I needed food. I would need to get something to eat to have energy to hike back. I held the string in my hand, its innocence turning sinister. I set it aside as I struggled to fix my pack. The backpack bottom was ripped out but the straps remained in fine condition so I began stitching the pack together as well as I could using a tent patch kit I had brought.

After repairing the pack I turned to the thin string. I fashioned a noose. And another. I spent the rest of the day setting snares. Afraid the bear or coyotes would come to this site because of the dehydrated food and its seasonings spread in the dirt, I decided to move down the trail a bit and return for the snares in the morning.

The new site was similar. A tree lined rugged campsite. Sun drenched sweat burned my eyes. I retreated into the shade. It had been a long day. I wished I were beside the lake to take a dip. Sitting on the cool ground I thought of Cari. Her defeated soul laying on the hospital bed unable to lift her head. Yearning for the last year to be reversed or changed somehow.

Though the bear had been a setback this was what I needed. I wanted her here. I wanted her to feel the relaxing atmosphere of nature. I slept little that night because of the bizarre sounds of wilderness. My groggy eyes opened to the early pink morning sunlight. All the horrifying sounds were soon reduced to tiny humorous examples of perception. As I walked to the snares I inhaled the clean air. Birds fluttered past and rabbits rushed across the trail. I checked and dismantled the first, deciding to try to get back to the car today. It would be a long trip but I was almost out of food. I approached the second snare and could hear rustling. The rabbit was medium sized. Afraid. Violently trying to escape as I came closer. I walked within ten yards of it and it tried to hide. Noose around its neck and front arm. It cowered in the dirt and grass.

Thirty-One

I remember killing my first mammal at twelve, a squirrel with my pellet gun in the back yard of our house. I hadn't really planned on having to approach death then just trying to see how good a shot I was. I had been very close to it. Having earned its trust by walking around him nearly each day. I betrayed him by aiming and firing at its head dropping him from a tree, he twitched in a spiral. It had been torn between life and death, wanting to live and fighting beyond reason to stay alive. He never had a choice. I walked over to it, tears in my eyes. Its eyes cold fading. I didn't touch him, I left him for my dog. I didn't have the heart or knowledge then to do anything with it.

I remembered those eyes as I realized I must make this swift. As painless as possible. I found a thick sturdy branch and grabbed the rabbit by the rear legs. It squealed. I raised the stick and let it fall to the base of its neck. Its body once tense now spasmed and went limp. It was warm. I didn't look at it. I didn't want to see his face.

Sorry, I had to do this. I have to eat. Thank you.

Setting it down on the ground I let the blood coagulate for thirty minutes or so. I got out my knife. Shiny cold clean blade. The rabbit's fur was soft. I held it gently as though an expensive gift. I placed the knife blade on its neck. And with the palm of my hand hit the spine of the knife. The neck cracked but did not sever. Again. A jolt shot through my hand.

I looked down at the separated head. I tried to avoid the eyes but like a curious child I had to look. Glassy. Helpless. Empty. For a moment I sat and looked at the carcass. Headless, still adorned with fur, the corpse appeared disturbing. Unappetizing. I cut the skin above the spine. Pulling in opposite directions the skin peeled away revealing soft pink flesh. Taking my knife, I cut off his feet. Another deep crunch as the small knife broke bone. Burying the head and feet nearby I continued with the carcass.

Taking a pinch of flesh around its stomach I made a cut. Slicing along his belly allowing me to remove its entrails. Organs. Stomach. Intestines. Bladder. Kidneys. Lungs. Heart. The white tail and anus were all left to remove. Two incisions on either side of the tail. I removed them leaving the carcass as just a shell and now just meat. It made it easy to wave off any further emotion. Now ready to cook I prepared a spit by mounting a couple y-shaped branches over a fire and cooked it.

Eating rabbit and beans that night was a reminder how life can be at once devastating then wonderful. Again I thanked the rabbit for sacrificing itself so I could gain energy to move forward the next day. Staring up at the Milky Way my stomach full, I took out Dmitri's flask and took a swig. The fire smoldered near my blistered feet and I fell asleep.

Thirty-Two

Stomach still full in the morning, the sun rose over mountains. Yellow pink hues cast across rocks and foliage. The air crisp and cool, casting steam from my mouth. I gathered my pack and rolled up the sleeping bag and pulled camp. The bottom of the pack grew unstable after riding five miles on my back. Sagging, nearly spilling all my gear. Having no other choice I stopped. I looked at the pack and decided that a hobo pack slung over a stick would be the best transport option. I found a suitable stick and attached the packs straps. Draped it. Tied it tighter against the stick with my remaining rope.

I walked the rest of the trail. Mostly a refreshing downhill. Feet throbbing. Legs and body tired and burning, I felt a huge relief as I reached the car. I sat in the seat for an hour thinking about the trip. I would miss this but I headed for home. Saddened each mile I drove away from this nature I had fallen for. I hoped someday to return and perhaps share it with someone. My mind felt good. Content. Once on the road I became nauseous and had a mild headache. I stopped and ate a burger and got some water. I drove an hour and had to pull over. The vomit mixed with the dry dirt and grass as cars rushed by. My joy was replaced with an anxiety and fear that the rabbit had some disease. Or maybe it was just the shock of eating the greasy burger. I felt better but the headache persisted. As I neared Baumgras it had gone. I was tired but ready to see Cari and Frank and get back to work. I got back to my apartment and went to sleep.

The next morning I called Frank. He asked about the trip and I told him about everything. I met him at his place after he got out of school. I got to there just before he got home. He pulled the Charger in the drive. I followed him inside.

It's strange Frank. On the way over here I felt like everything was so over-stimulating. I can see in people's faces their ideas, thoughts, pain, happiness. But what does it all mean? I grew up believing in god you know, but I don't even know if that's true.

Dughall, you're on this journey, you've had a lot of shit happen and I can't answer it but maybe you could read some stuff. I've found that reading psychology and philosophy really helps. You're welcome to borrow any of my books.

He waved his hand at the large floor to ceiling bookshelf next to us. I grabbed a book. A man's old wise face reflected frozen, head bald with glasses. I nodded, reading the back. Unable to focus on the words in the moment, I said, Maybe this will help but I think I might need to talk to a therapist or something

That could be good for you. It might help you understand a little of what you are feeling, he said.

I don't know.

I stared at the bookshelves for a moment.

I'm gonna go. I've got to go see Cari.

He nodded as I stood. I held out my hand and we shook. I left Frank's place feeling no better. I got in the Chevelle and went to see Cari. As I pulled into a parking space, I felt the excitement of seeing her. I shut the car off and slammed the door. I walked in and toward Cari's room. A nurse smiled at the reception desk.

Her room was lit by the open curtains and photos of me, Dmitri and her family sat on a desk. One side of the bed was shoved up against the wall the way she liked it. At first I only saw her hair strewn across the pillow. Her head slowly rose, revealing her face. It was thinner than before my trip. Her eyes and cheeks sunken, lips dry pale pink. They did not smile. A feeding tube lay across her cheek into her nose.

Hey you, she said, eyes drowsy. Voice tired.

Hey. How are you?

I walked over to her. Took her hand. Her skin was soft and cold and bony like an elderly woman's. I held it with both hands. She squeezed. I wanted to reveal to her everything I had learned about myself. Inspire her. Invigorate her to rise like Lazarus. Instead she half-smiled. Cheeks barely moved.

How do I look?

I looked down at the floor embarrassed I had asked. I felt her eyes still looking at me.

I want to die Dughall, but they put this feeding tube in today.

I looked at her somber face. Her eyes even looked different. Weary. She shook her head.

They don't understand. There's nothing left for me here. It's all empty and sad. I lost my best friend, my brother. I killed Francis. I watched blood pump out of his body. I saw his eyes Dughall. They were so empty. I wish I could undo it and somehow talk him out of shooting me. But I can't.

Tears streamed down her sunken cheeks. Her hand grew limp as her body trembled. I held it as she sobbed. The room was silent. I felt an eerie cold as if any moment Dmitri would appear. But there was nothing but the emptiness of the room. I struggled to maintain composure as my own sadness resurfaced. A headache came too. My eyes grew blurry but not from tears. This hadn't happened before.

I know, that's how I feel. I feel that way too. I wish I could change all this but I want you to know that I'm here for you. I always have been.

It's not the same!

Her tone was sharp. I wanted to get up and walk away. Leave her there and take care of this headache and blurry eyes. But I didn't. I sat there as her sobs subsided. She looked at me.

Dughall. Go live your life without me. I can't

stand you seeing me like this.

Her eyes moist and swollen. I shook my head.

I can't Cari. I can't just leave you like this. I want to help you.

I don't want your help. I don't want any help.

I sat there on the edge of the bed and held her hand. I looked at the pictures of me and her and Dmitri. And back at Cari lying in bed with a tube on her face. I leaned over. Kissed her forehead.

I love you Cari. I'll always be here for you.

She did not look at me and did not speak for a minute or so and then said, I love you too, Dughall.

She sat up and hugged me. Kissed my cheek. I walked out and got in the Chevelle. I turned onto the street back toward Frank's house.

Thirty-Three

I was glad he was still home. It would be good to talk to someone and not sit alone in my apartment sifting through old photos and memories.

Dughall, what's up?

I went and saw Cari.

How was it?

Good . . . I mean . . . not really good. She's not looking well.

Frank nodded, staring at me intently.

She looked horrible. I just wanted to go back and fix everything, bring her back to her old self. But I couldn't. I can't. It's all my fault. I should have been there to defend her and Dmitri. If I would've been there none of this would've happened.

Frank looked me in the eye.

You can't say that. Maybe you would've died. How would that have affected her? What if you and Dmitri had both died? I know you want her to be okay and go back to how things were but you can't. It's her life. You've just got to continue to be there. There's no sense in blaming yourself for any of it.

My head pounded. I wanted to get up and run away. I didn't want to hear this. I didn't want to think about her anymore. His comments seemed like every clichéd dialogue in any book or movie. I wanted to laugh them off and tell him it's all a fucking lie. But as much as I hated to admit that it was a cliché, I knew it was all true. I looked at him.

Yeah, you're right. I just want her to be alright. I still love her. I think it's that I had such a great experience backpacking and I want her to share that with me. Maybe it's my own hope that she'll come out of this a more beautiful woman. Changed. Still in love with me. I think that's maybe what I want but I know it's unlikely.

We want to see the good in all situations, but you're a realist. You want her to heal and love you but you also know that will never happen. You see these two sides of the situation which is something you do often. See many sides to things. It's a rare talent. But it also divides you. You can't have it all Dughall.

I took it in for a moment and smiled. It was all true. Frank understood. Possibly even more than I understood myself. We sat in silence. Frank nodded to himself and picked up his book. I sat in the chair noticing my headache had subsided. Feeling a great relief I picked up a lighter and lit a cigarette.

As I was driving home that night, my headache worsened. I tried to ignore it as a stress headache but it remained almost constant over the next couple days. It was there each morning. Sometimes followed by vomiting. Some days I would vomit multiple times and my energy was low. I realized it was absurd to ignore any longer and scheduled a doctor's appointment with Dr. Masterson.

Dr. Masterson had been my doctor since I was a kid but as I walked into the office my heartbeat thumped. Mouth grew dry. It was bright with white fluorescent lights. White walls. I felt blinded. I walked up to the desk. Nervousness grew as the receptionist smiled up at me.

Hi! How can I help you?

I've got an appointment with Dr. Masterson.

I massaged my hands together like a nervous evil mastermind.

What was your name?

What?

Your name?

Dughall.

Oh! Yes! If you'll just have a seat the doctor will be right with you.

I sat there for thirty minutes. Every once in a while the receptionist would look up at me and smile. I kneaded my hands. As my nervousness led to boredom a nurse called my name. I followed her. I wanted to tell her I wasn't worried about my weight or height or eyesight. I was having headaches and puking every day. I didn't want a fucking physical. She left me in a room to wait for the doctor. More waiting. My hands sweating I just wanted the doctor to show up so I could go home and sleep.

Dughall?

I explained my symptoms. He nodded his head

only stopping to take my heartbeat and check my lungs. Asking me to breathe as the icy button of his stethoscope touched my bare skin. I breathed in and out. He remained silent for a while until telling me he would be right back. I waited again. I puked in the trash can. He returned and told me they needed to do some tests.

We'll have to take some blood today. And I'll get you a date and time of the x-rays and imaging scans we'll have to do.

What do you think it is?

I hate to make any assumptions this early Dughall. We'll do these tests and go from there, alright?

I nodded. He raised his eyebrows seriously as he patted my shoulder before walking out. I waited again. In the interim I got the information for the other tests. The phlebotomist came in stabbed my arm. I didn't watch. After they told me they would get back to me within a few days, I went home. Worried.

Thirty-Four

The next day I went back to work. All the guys at the shop asked if I was all right. But I didn't know. And they just said, It's probably nothing. I shrugged and looked at my work order. A 1976 Chevy V8 2WD truck. The owner wanted engine and suspension work. I scraped the old crusty dried silicone and cork from the valve covers. Hands greasy. Oily. Put new valve covers on with fresh continuous beads of silicone. Wiped the grease off them.

Adjusted the air mixture screws on the carburetor and pushed the throttle to make sure fuel sprayed properly from the tiny nozzles in the carburetor. I was getting ready to start the engine when my boss came over.

You've got a call Dughall.

Alright. Tell'em I'll be there in a sec.

I wiped the grease and oil off my hands. I stared into the engine bay. My eyes focused on the metal and mechanical parts. I cleaned my hands longer than necessary and took a breath. I didn't want to hear what the doctor had to say. Walked to the office and picked up the phone. Sniffles came from the other line. They were familiar. Cari's mother.

Mrs. Miller?

I didn't need to ask what was wrong.

Dughall . . . Cari's gone. She died this morning.

Across the line I could see her face drawn. Weary.

Wrinkles more pronounced as her mouth flexed in a mournful frown. Eyes squinted. Squeezing out tears. I had seen that face before. It had been my own. It had been Cari's. And Jessica's. It was a truthful sadness shared in the darkest most fearful moments. I sat down in the office chair. Looked around. There was no one in the lobby.

What happened?

She had a heart attack. Doctors say that the feeding tube was a shock to her body after not eating for so long. I can't believe she's gone Dughall.

She had wanted to die. The doctors may say a heart attack killed her but this is what she had wanted. I felt a peace. I knew Cari meant not for me to mourn but smile. She wasn't hurting anymore. I talked to her mother a little longer. She would let me know when the visitation was and all the details. I told her I would see her soon. Hung up.

I sat in the office for ten minutes. My boss came in. Asked if everything was alright. I nodded.

Everything is fine.

I walked back to the truck. Pumped the gas. Started it. Revved the engine. The RPMs rose smoothly. I got out to look for oil leaking from the valve covers. There was none. I shut it off and put the lift arms under the frame. Raised the lift and worked on the suspension.

I went home after work. The first thing I saw was a blanket Cari had left on the couch. I picked it up and held it. Set it down. Went to the fridge and grabbed a beer. I thought about her as I stood in the kitchen. I saw her face. It smiled at all the times we had held hands and laughed, all the moments we shared on the Gulf Coast. It didn't feel real. She couldn't be gone like that. I felt my eyes grow warm and my head began to throb again. I lay down with the blanket on the couch.

I tried to sleep but between my thoughts and headache I couldn't. I saw my parents. Jessica Hall. I saw Dmitri and Francis. And Cari. All glassy eyed and cold. A fearful emptiness shivered through my body imagining feeling nothing, knowing less and leaving familiarity behind. I held the blanket against my chest like a child and fell asleep.

Thirty-Five

I stopped by Frank's place after work the next day.

It all happens for a reason Dughall. It's a tired saying but it's true.

I know, I just . . . I just wanted it to be different you know? I wish I could've been there with her. I should've been there.

You were there for her. And she wanted you to live your life. She loved you.

Frank's voice lent a finality to the conversation with these three words. For a moment I sat reflecting on my life. The deaths of parents, grandparents, a friend, a lover, a competitor, a stranger.

I guess you're right. I love her and wish she could have healed like I wanted for her. But she didn't want that. She wanted . . .

I stared at the clean, low pile carpet.

Have you written anything lately?

I shook my head.

Not really. I should though.

He nodded. We both lit cigarettes. Sat there in silence. Mrs. Miller had called me today and told me the visitation would be tomorrow. Friday. The funeral Saturday. I remembered Dmitri's funeral. The sadness. I sucked on my cigarette. Smoke filled my lungs. Spit it out. Steady stream like Dmitri used to do.

You talk to Vicky yet? Frank said.

No. I need to though.

Yeah. You should call her.

I nodded and took out my phone. There was a missed call and voice mail. I'd listen later. I dialed Vicky.

Hello?

Hey Vicky. It's Dughall. How are you?

Doin good! You?

Alright I guess. I've got something to, ah, tell you. It's hard for me to say this, but Cari's gone.

Gone? She left?

No. She died yesterday. Heart attack.

Oh my god Dughall! Oh my god! Dughall, that's horrible. Oh my god . . .

Her voice shaky.

I hope you can make it, but the visitation is tomorrow and funeral Saturday.

Yes. I'll be there Dughall. Are you okay Dughall?

I'm alright. It's rough of course but I'm sitting here with Frank now.

Good. Tell him I said hi.

I will. Let me know when you'll get in town. We can meet up.

Sure. Take care of yourself Dughall. You need anything. Anything at all, call me okay.

I will.

We said goodbye and Frank and I sat there in the

chairs in his living room. Surrounded by books of knowledge. We sat and smoked until midnight. We did not say anything. At midnight I got up.

I've got to work tomorrow.

He nodded. Put out his cigarette. Came over and gave me a hug.

See you tomorrow night, man. Be careful on your way home.

I will.

I waved and walked out to the Chevelle. I looked up. The stars and moon were clear. No clouds. The air was crisp and chilly. I looked at the empty street. Straight grey concrete strip. The hood of the Chevelle reflected the moon. I lit a cigarette and stood in the driveway against the Chevelle. Tossed cigarette on driveway. Squashed it. I got in. Pulled out my phone. Listened to the voicemail.

Dughall, this is Dr. Masterson's office. We would like to schedule some additional tests. If you could call us back as soon as possible, that would be great.

I tossed the phone into the passenger seat and drove the cold empty streets back to my apartment.

Thirty-Six

I did not sleep that night. I lay thinking. Crying. Eyes staring at the dark shadowed ceiling. Sometimes I closed them to relive a memory that now seemed so far away, like a dream. I longed for them, I wanted to recapture and relive them all. Those fleeting memories of Cari and Dmitri. In the early morning before sunrise, another headache struck me. Throbbing pain, my vision blurry. I called in to work. Around 8 am I finally fell to sleep and woke at noon. Felt somehow rested and the headache was gone.

It was a beautiful day so I got up and got in the Chevelle. I drove gravel roads and found myself approaching the driveway to Cari and Dmitri's parent's house. I intended to drive past but noticed a figure walking across the road to check the mailbox. It was Mr. Miller. I knew I had to stop and I began thinking of ways to get out of going inside. The memory would be too much. I stopped the car next to him as he waved. He smiled but his face was tight with sadness.

Dughall! So glad to see ya.

Good to see you too Mr. Miller. How are you guys holding up?

He looked down for a moment then lifted his head nodding.

Yeah, we are about as good as we can be. I'm

handling it better than the missus. But at least we can see all the love everyone had for Cari. Want to come in?

He looked me in the eye with the same tearful sadness that had been in Cari's the last time I saw her. My stomach turned. Excited and nervous. I hesitated but knew I must say yes.

Yeah sure I could go in for a minute.

Pulling the car in the drive was the most natural feeling I'd had in almost a year. It felt right to be here. The house was unchanged. Flowers lining the sidewalk. The garden green with life and the trees towering behind were all the same as every time I had been here. I got out barely able to hear the gravel crunch above my heartbeat. Mr. Miller walked slowly up the drive. Head down. Looking up as he neared, he nodded.

Come on in.

I walked behind him. The screen door creaked. The smell of cooking chicken, biscuits and mashed potatoes tickled my nose. But I was too nervous to think about food.

There were people there that I did not know. They glanced at me and looked away. Each of their faces somber. Emotionless. Mrs. Miller approached me. Eyes filled with tears. She hugged me holding my shoulders like every proud mother.

Oh Dughall . . .

We stayed like that for a moment. She hugging me

tight, face in my chest. I hugged her back. I could hear Mr. Miller telling the people that I was Cari's fiancé. They said, Okay. Or, Oh, I wondered who that was. I looked down at the top of Mrs. Miller's head. It was the same shape and color as Cari's. She raised her head. Eyes met mine. She put her hands on my shoulders. I gave her a half smile.

Come here, she said.

I followed her into Cari's bedroom. It still smelled like her. Pictures of her and I and Dmitri were everywhere. Mrs. Miller walked to a box on the bed. She opened it and took out a picture in a frame. She held it up to me. It was a picture of Cari and Dmitri and I sitting on a couch laughing. We looked very young.

This was her favorite picture. It was from three years ago. She always had this close to her.

I nodded.

She wanted you to have this box too, Dughall. She told me that if anything happened to her that this was yours. I put some other things in here for you too.

She walked over to me and hugged me again.

Stay in here as long as you like, Dughall.

She walked out and I stood for a moment. I went to the box and looked at the photo for a long while before placing it carefully in the box. I closed the lid and walked into the bathroom. My head was throbbing again. I looked at my face. My eyes were swollen and my image seemed to throb rhythmically.

I opened the medicine cabinet. I plucked past bottles. Prozac. Doxepin. St. John's Wort. Omega 3. Most were full. Grabbing an ibuprofen bottle I poured four into my hand and dumped them onto my tongue. I turned on the tap and cupped my hand. Filled it with water. Before it drained I scooped it into my mouth washing down the pills. Swallowing it as water dripped between the cracks of my fingers. I looked back at my reflection.

How different I looked. Older. Even more than six months ago. Vague thin lines had begun to form next to my eyes and around my mouth. My eyes looked back with immediacy. My lips seemed to smile back at me. I turned away. Picked up the box. Turned off the lights. Soft voices came from the living room. Mr. and Mrs. Miller were talking to several people. I set the box down by the door. Walked over and tapped Mr. Miller on the shoulder.

I'm gonna go, Mr. Miller. I've got to meet up with Frank and Vicky.

It was good to see you Dughall. See you all later?

Yes sir.

I nodded and we shook hands as Mrs. Miller came over to hug me. We said goodbye and I picked up the box and walked to the Chevelle.

My head throbbed and my mind swirled as I drove home. I pulled the key from the ignition and I sat replaying each word and glance. I walked in to the apartment and set the box down by the door. I would look at it later. My headache had subsided but my vision was blurry again so I called Frank to pick me up.

We met Vicky and Brent at Hadley's BBQ. We walked in. Vicky waved at us from a table. She stood up as we walked over. Hugged me.

Oh Dughall. I'm so sorry.

No one said anything as we sat down. I looked over at Brent and nodded. He returned the gesture.

Brent, how've you been? Frank said.

Vicky and I looked over at Frank and Brent.

Good Frank. How about you?

Good. I graduate in April. Looking forward to being finished.

That's great. What was your degree again?

Major in Computer Science. Minor in English Lit.

Nice. A lot of opportunities right now.

Frank nodded. I looked across the table at Vicky.

It's good to see you. It's been a while.

She smiled.

It has. But it's good to see both of you too.

The waitress came and took our order.

You guys aren't engaged yet? I said.

Nope. Still waiting.

Vicky nodded in the direction of Brent. He rolled his eyes. Frank and I laughed. And it felt good to laugh. We smiled and ate and drank.

We all got in Frank's Charger and pulled onto the

Boulevard toward the funeral home. Frank gunned it a little as pulled out. The rear of the car swung out slightly.

Whoa! Brent said.

I looked back at Brent. He was gripping Vicky's hand. She grinned.

You ever ride in a muscle car Brent?

No. Never have.

I looked over at Frank. There was a slight upward curve to his lips. He stared straight ahead.

You better hold on.

He just looked at me as I glanced back at him. His mouth hung open and his eyes were large behind his glasses. Frank downshifted and floored it. The Charger's low gurgle became a loud whaaaaaa.

Holy shit! You guys are crazy!

We laughed as Frank let off the gas and shifted gears. We pulled in to the funeral home. There were more cars than I thought there would be.

The door felt heavy as I pulled it open. I let everyone go ahead before me. The light was dim. Not dark but not bright. The hallway led to the visitation room. I had already told myself I would not go in. I didn't want to see her. I followed Frank and Vicky and Brent to the door. And stopped. They kept walking but Vicky looked back to see if I was coming. She walked over to me.

You're not going in?

No. I don't want to see her.

She nodded and stood there next to me. Held my hand. People walked by. Some I knew. Some said hi. We said hi back. Frank and Brent walked out. Brent looked at Vicky's hand holding mine. I let go.

Thought you followed us in there.

I looked at Frank and shook my head.

Mr. and Mrs. Miller asked about you. I told them you were here.

Maybe they'll come out here soon, I said.

We stood there and finally they came out.

Dughall, we've been waiting for you, Mrs. Miller said, Did you want to come in and look at her.

No, not now.

They both nodded and gave me a hug. The three of us. We separated and Mr. and Mrs. Miller looked at us.

Thank you all for coming. It means so much to us.

Vicky gave Mrs. Miller a hug and said, She meant so much to each us, we had to come.

We walked out the way we had come. Took Brent and Vicky back to their car. Frank took me back to my Chevelle at the garage. I opened the glove box and rubbed Dmitri's flask with my thumb.

Thirty-Seven

I met Frank, Vicky and Brent at Pancake House the next morning. I recalled the day after the accident. It felt so recent yet so distant. I thought of Jessica Hall. Her face screaming. Arms wide. Maybe that accident changed it all. If it hadn't happened how would it all be different? I didn't know. And I didn't want to bring this up now.

We sat there. Brent and Frank and I wearing suits. White shirts and black coats and ties. Vicky in a plain black dress. We ate eggs. Pancakes. Hashbrowns. We smiled. Laughed. Listened. Vicky talked of their life in St. Louis and school and all their favorite things to do. We talked about Cari and Dmitri and all the times in high school. All the times after. The waiter took our plates and we sat there for a while. Reminiscing. And we left.

We got in my Chevelle. Brent and Vicky in the back. Frank smoked in the passenger seat. I looked in the rearview mirror.

Brent, you like donuts?

He hesitated a moment.

Yeah, I like donuts.

Alright.

Oh dammit, Brent! That's one of Dmitri's old tricks. Hold on! Vicky said as I pulled out of the parking space. Into an open part of the lot. I pushed the pedal to the floor. Engine screamed. Tires spun. Spewing smoke in a circular trail behind us as the car swung wildly around in a three-sixty. Frank held onto the a-pillar and Brent fell into Vicky's lap.

Holy crap, man. I don't like donuts anymore.

We laughed and drove to the funeral home. Walked into the chapel. The open casket sat in the front of the room. Mr. and Mrs. Miller were there with other relatives. They told us to sit with them in the front row. We put our coats on the pews. Stood there talking. Talking to people we didn't know. People we did know. I kept my back to the casket. I wanted to see her. But knew the memories may be too much.

I felt Mrs. Miller's hand on my arm.

Dughall, would you walk with me to look at her?

I took a breath.

Yes, I'll go with you.

And we went to the casket. As if a slow-panning camera had replaced my vision, her body appeared before me. Pale. Thin. But not as thin as I had last seen her. She was beautiful. And looked peaceful. I felt my eyes warm. Mrs. Miller sniffled next to me. Her face puffy. Eyes red. I imagined this was what Jessica Hall's mother had looked like too. I expected Cari to get up at any moment. Hug me. Kiss me. I could not look any longer. My eyes stared at the carpet as Mrs. Miller wept into my arm. We stood for a while. People came to pay respects. I sat down on the pew.

The service commenced. I do not remember

much of what was said or the prayers or any of it. And it was over. Frank and I and two of Cari's uncles carried the casket to the hearse. We began the procession to the cemetery. Nobody said anything as we drove through town. The exhaust of the Chevelle echoed in a low garble against the pavement and buildings. Everything seemed quiet. At the cemetery, a cold wind blew across our heads. Words were spoken and lost, everyone focusing on the casket and hole beneath it.

The minister gestured and read from his bible. Women dabbed their eyes with handkerchiefs and tissues. I stood with my hands in front of me. Vicky stood at my right. Rubbed my back occasionally. Frank fidgeted on my left. I knew he wanted a cigarette. The service ended but I stood there. Head pounded with a headache. My vision grew blurry. I handed Frank my keys.

Drive us home will you?

Yeah sure. You okay?

Just a headache. Nothing to worry about.

He drove us back to the restaurant and Vicky and Brent got in her car. Frank and I stayed in mine. They followed us. And he dropped me off, gave me my keys.

You going to be okay man? he said.

I'll be fine. Just need to sleep it off.

He nodded and squeezed my shoulder and said, Give me a call soon.

Sure thing.

I walked into the apartment and looked at the box. I was tired but I wanted to know what was in it. I opened it and thumbed through many different pictures of Cari and I. There were some small trinkets I had always remembered in Cari's room. At the bottom was a stack of papers. I flipped through them. Poems. I spent much of the night reading and toward the bottom of the stack there was a short one written on a small piece of paper.

Dughall
Constant thoughts of you
Always in my heart
I miss you and I love you.

I held the paper between my fingers. I took the picture of her and I and Dmitri and put it on my nightstand and tucked the poem in the corner below her face. I lay on my side and looked at the picture.

Thirty-Eight

Monday morning I called the doctor's office to schedule more appointments. Between the tests and increasing feelings of fatigue, I missed work regularly over the next couple of weeks. My headaches worsened, sometimes extending for an entire day. The last imaging scan was completed and I felt a relief. Maybe I would soon know what was wrong and what could be done. I waited impatiently and finally got a call to set up another appointment. I sat in the room. Waiting. Dr. Masterson finally walked in. He was not smiling as before.

Dughall. Have a seat.

I sat down sensing an uneasiness and a tenderness that I hadn't noticed in Dr. Masterson before.

Well as you know, we got your test results back. I'm afraid it looks like you have a brain tumor called Gliomatosis Cerebri.

The words felt heavy and I did not believe them.

It's a rather rare form that, due to its precarious position in your brain is inoperable. There are treatments that we could discuss if . . .

He grew silent then and must have realized I was tuning out. For the first time since my vomiting began I genuinely wanted to puke. My stomach felt like it were being pulled out of my body by a crane. I looked at a poster of the human body on the wall. Dr. Masterson lowered his head reluctantly and fidgeted with the manilla folder and papers inside. He pulled out brain scans. He said something but I did not hear. I looked at the image of my brain. I could see the mass in the center. I looked over at him.

How long do I have?

It sounded a distant question but one in which I did not fear the answer. I felt strangely content.

Without treatment I would give you around ninety days. With radiation and chemotherapy, which I would strongly recommend, you would have between three to eighteen months. If you chose gamma knife surgery as well I would extend that prognosis to three years. It would all depend on your treatment. Dughall try the options, you are young, your body can fight this.

He sounded serious. Like my father had when he had scolded me for my first speeding ticket.

I looked into his eyes with a bit of sadness. I already knew what I would say.

I put in my two weeks' notice the day after the diagnosis. My parents had left me a substantial amount of money from their insurance. I figured I could live off that until I died. I didn't tell anyone at work other than my boss that I was leaving. Nor did I tell Vicky or Frank or Cari's family. Instead I wrote. I carried a notebook with me wherever I was and wrote whatever came to me. I needed to leave something behind.

I entitled the notebook The Life of Dughall Martin. I wrote poetry and stories and short expository pieces. The expository, philosophical ones were my favorites. There was one I read repeatedly. Its words were nearly unknown to me. I didn't remember writing it but it was on the page in my hand.

> The father feverishly waves, welted fingers covered in blood. Teeth crooked. Yellow. Cracked. Feet growing vines from boots onto sidewalk making each step fastidiously forward, leaning, lending us his sweat softly telling us, Go forward, into this, into that, that which I did not discover. His directions lost on youth.
>
> Hands in pockets, head down, the beggars walk into gardens of grapes. Smelling flowery broken branches and entrusting feet to ground, coin filled pockets drooping and heavy, fleetingly wish it were their heart. Even they understand the burden of a heavy, full heart, the compassion, brokenness, sadness, empathy. Too much. They know this, they do not dwell. They allow their pockets to break, planting seeds for the father's children.

The father gathers grapes above all this, laboring, lustful for freedom. Each time a coin is found the father mourns, crying into collection plates tears flushing gallons of sewery, shit-stuffed water down into his own stomach, rotgut filled with gutrot, intestines filled with the pus of voluminous gnashing fixated ransomed fellows, shoved deep in the recess of introspective unknown minds. And the father dies, for each of us, some strange unholy, empty death. The union of all the world's sorrow, troubled and killed, raped to the end of earth vomiting into space this father's soul. Still in death, his hands bleed from swinging hammers and axes, eyes forever wet in sorrow for you and me and everyone.

But know this child, he is not god, a god or deity, he is everything wonderful that will ever happen and after you forget, he will die this death. But you will forget. It is meant to be, this death. Everyone knows this. Few feel it, but it's there, dying to find you, wistful that you will remember, wishing wisdom will reign in your heart. But you just can't care that much. You never will.

Each time I read this, I recalled Jessica Hall. Her face death white. Dmitri lying dead on ground, blood pooled on chest. Cari, dead in bed with mouth open and dried saliva on her chin. Everything tinted gray after reading. I drove the melancholy streets lost in the smoke of sadness as sulphuric fumes drifted around me. Amidst this doom I gave people little chance. I did not want their help. I wanted this sadness to myself.

Thirty-Nine

My final week of work was enveloped in this sadness. A few people knew I was leaving now. They voiced their concern for me. But I did not want this. I was ready to go. What use was it fighting? On the last day of work I decided to tell Frank. I wanted to tell Vicky as well, but did not want to devastate her. They were the closest thing to family I had left.

I called Frank and met him that night. It was a Friday and I don't suspect he thought it too much out of the ordinary. I was nervous. The basement had recently been renovated and it smelled like new plaster and wood. I took a deep breath as I walked in. I sat in the recliner across from him. He lit a cigarette.

So what's up Dughall? You find another job yet?

I shook my head.

No. I've got something to tell you Frank.

He took a drag, waiting for me to continue.

I'm dying.

He slowly exhaled white curling smoke. His eyes studied my face. I wanted to laugh and pretend it was fake. A joke. But I couldn't. It would not be fair to him. He and Vicky were all I had now. They had to know.

Seriously?

Yeah.

I told him everything. Brain scans. Blurred vision.

The doctor's visit. He didn't nod. He only smoked. Face remained calm. He slowly got up and pulled a ragged T.S. Eliot poetry book from the bookshelf and fingered the yellowed pages.

My grandfather was a good man. Fought in World War II. He wanted to be a writer and got a job at the newspaper here in Baumgras and had the chance to interview T.S. Eliot. He signed this book for my grandfather. My grandfather gave me that book the year I was born. But my father did not give it to me until I was seventeen. He told me that I was a man now and could take care of it.

Frank stopped for a moment, closing the book gently and placed it back on the shelf. He took out another cigarette, lit it and sat down. He looked over at me through the smoke. He reminded me of Dmitri. Quiet pensive eyes calculating the next word. The next story.

My grandfather died of a brain tumor when I was two years old. He knew I would not remember him. They had given him only a few months to live.

Cigarette in his mouth, eyes squinting, he reached under the table next to him and pulled out a large plastic box. He took another puff and set the cigarette on the ashtray. Opening the box he glanced up at me.

In those months and years after the diagnosis he never got a second opinion. He figured he would die when he would die. He spent as much time with me as he could but of course I don't remember him and he must've known this because this box is full of letters he wrote me. Some are happy. Some sad, but they all reveal who he was and where, on the day that he wrote the note, he was emotionally. I probably know him better through these than if he had lived a long life. He left a legacy you know? It wasn't a massive estate or anything but he gave me something to treasure and that's what really matters. Affecting people in a genuine authentic way. They remember you then. Even if it's just one person.

I nodded as he put the lid back on the box and placed it back in its spot. He picked up his cigarette as if my revelation had been known all along and he had been waiting for me to tell him. I took out a cigarette. I searched for a lighter or matches. I looked at Frank.

You got a light?

He nodded, tossing me a lighter. Our eyes met through the smoke. He smiled.

Forty

The Chevelle's low voice hummed over the large Midwest hills that interrupted the plains of Kansas and Iowa. St. Louis wasn't a far drive. An hour and a half. But it felt longer. Though Frank was dealing with my illness in his own internal way I knew this would not be so with Vicky. I thought of turning back. Maybe never talking to her again. My hands shook as I arrived at her and Brent's apartment. I sat in my car staring at the dash.

An apartment door opened. She looked more beautiful than I remembered as she ran down the stairs to my car.

Dughall! I'm so glad to see you!

I got out of the car as an old man does. I was in no hurry to tell her my news.

Me too. How is everything? How is Brent?

Oh he's good. He's at work now which is normal. You know he just started this job and everything. He has a lot going on right now so I'm not giving him too much of a hard time.

Her excitement and love for Brent made me remember Cari. I nodded as she looked at me. A serious concerned face.

How are you?

I'm alright I guess. A lot has happened since I saw you last. So I don't know. I think I'm okay but sometimes it's hard to tell. I mean, I miss them. Dmitri and Cari. It's strange to think about her being gone. It's hard sometimes.

A silence followed. I had nothing more to say and she was unable to offer anything. We both looked down at the concrete.

You want to come inside?

I nodded and followed her.

The apartment was tidy and smelled fresh. Knowing Vicky I imagined it was always like this. Pictures of her and Brent covered the walls. On a long thin table were pictures of me, Vicky, Dmitri and Cari. It felt long ago. Almost as if it never happened. My eyes lingered on Cari's smiling face. How gorgeous she was. A hand touched my shoulder.

Those were the good times weren't they?

Vicky took my head in both hands and lowered it to her lips. She held my face steadying my eyes on hers. I wanted to kiss her though I knew I shouldn't. I resisted but felt something then for her that I never had before. We stood for a while staring at the photos before sitting on the spotless white couch.

So what brings you here Dughall?

I . . . have something to tell you. And it's hard, you know, after all this stuff that's happened to have this happen. But, well, I have a brain tumor. And my prognosis is less than a year, probably sooner.

Her body shifted. Her mouth opened. Face

looked as if I had slapped her.

Are you serious? I mean you got this checked out and everything right? It's not like you self-diagnosed yourself or something?

I'm serious. My doctor ran about every test you can and showed me where the mass was and what it was.

You didn't get a second opinion or anything? Dughall, maybe you should. Would you get one for me? I mean maybe he's wrong. I'm sure he is, that can't be right can it? You're so young.

It's true. I have headaches every day and often vomit. Blurry vision too. I saw the brain scans and I believe it.

But Dughall you can't just go like that . . .

Her face configured into an unholy mess of passion and concern. She cried. I scooted over embracing her. Holding her head to my shoulder.

Brent arrived shortly after and I was glad he did. I felt something new for Vicky and I didn't know how to handle it. Brent's face was tired. Behind his glasses his eyes drooped. His tall well postured figure wilted. He glanced at me skeptically. I understood the glance. His eyes were the same as each of Vicky's past boyfriends. I was used to them. Vicky rushed to embrace, kiss him.

Hey babe.

I looked away from their smooch. Vicky glanced at me after. He looked at me. An awkward glance.

What is it? Vicky? Is everything alright?

She shook her head. I looked up at him.

I'm dying. I have an aggressive brain tumor.

Jesus. I'm sorry Dughall. I had no idea.

Vicky's face was buried in her hands now. I had an urge to laugh. Probably because of the tension and Brent's immediate change in attitude. Or maybe because I was nervous. Whatever it was I smiled. Brent's face dropped.

Are you joking?

I shook my head. My smile dropped away.

No I'm not. I'm just nervous talking about it.

He looked at me for a moment. Maybe he was sizing me up. Trying to see if I was bluffing. Hiding something. Maybe he knew I had wanted to kiss Vicky.

Brent looked at me. Then back at her. He nodded toward the bedroom.

Vicky I'm going to get changed.

Alright honey well go ahead.

He looked at me again.

Can I talk to you while I change?

She gave him a goofy smile and followed him into the room. I knew all too well the conversation. I had never really been nervous around any of her boyfriends. Maybe because we had such a unique relationship for so many years. Or maybe because I never looked at Vicky that way.

They walked back out of the bedroom. He in new clothes. Her eyes rested on the floor. His face stern. It was clear he was jealous. He didn't want me alone with her. He looked over at me. His eyes lingering. I held his gaze as he looked at me and spoke.

You want to go eat with us Dughall?

I almost said no. I wanted to say no. Vicky looked up at me over Brent's shoulder. Her eyes large. Eager.

Sure. I'll come.

We went to a Mexican restaurant. Conversation was kept to surface topics. Jobs. Family. Friends. No one mentioned the tension until Brent went to the restroom. Vicky smirked at me.

He doesn't want me hanging out with you alone. It makes him uncomfortable.

This sounds familiar, doesn't it? Every time you have a boyfriend they think I'm going to steal you away.

I know and I don't really care you know? You've been a friend for so long . . . my best friend and I'm not just going to let that go. Especially now that you're dying.

Even if something were to happen between us it's not like it would be long term . . .

Her cheeks flushed.

Dughall! Do not talk like that!

She dabbed her eyes with her napkin.

Sorry. We've never really had anything happen before anyway. Did you tell him that? Maybe if you told him he wouldn't care so much.

I glanced at the waitress as I said it. She nodded as

Brent came and sat back down. He looked at both of us.

Everything alright?

He stared at me as if in accusation. I nodded.

Everything is fine. I was just talking to Vicky about my tumor.

Vicky lifted her head high. Shoulders prepared for the weight of his glance. Brent looked down at his food. His face understood what had been spoken. It understood that Vicky was more independent than he thought. Maybe he was reorganizing his thoughts about me. Perhaps understanding the situation yet afraid of what could happen. After all a man is still a man and woman still woman until they die.

Forty-One

I left as soon as we got back to their apartment. I needed to think. Breathe. Distance myself. Maybe I shouldn't have visited. Maybe I shouldn't have told her anything and just died. The next few days I resigned that I would never see her again. It was best to honor their relationship, but I felt lonely. My apartment felt boring. Bleak. Melancholy. I had no job. I only had one friend left. Everyone else was gone. I needed to talk to Frank. I drove fast. He was in his chair. Reading. Smoking.

Frank, I need to talk to you about Vicky.

He slowly lowered his book. Eyes lingered on the page. Finishing the paragraph or scene before looking over the book at me.

What's going on?

I have feelings for her. I wanted to kiss her.

He raised his cigarette. Stared at me through the smoke. He took a couple drags before saying anything.

Really?

Yeah. I never thought of her this way before, Frank. I mean I always thought she was attractive but I never thought I would fall for her. She was always just a friend. I think she always felt this too. It was something we never talked about.

Yeah I never thought of you two as a couple either. Kind've like a Jack Kerouac-Carolyn Cassady relationship. You two just didn't fit romantically. I don't think anyone in our circle saw you guys that way. It was always you and Cari. But maybe now is the time. I mean Kerouac and Carolyn had their romantic relationship.

I guess that's true.

Maybe now you and her should give it a go.

I don't know. She's with Brent and I just don't want to screw up that relationship.

He nodded. I could tell he had nothing more to say. This was my decision. He hovered his cigarette over the ashtray and tapped it. Ash fluttered into the tray. His hand waved the cigarette as though a wand motioning toward me.

Speaking of Vicky, we've been talking and think it might be good to have you move in with me. I've got the basement which I never use. It's built as an apartment but I never wanted to deal with someone I didn't know living under me. It's got a small bar area with a sink that would work as a kitchen. I think it'd be good for you.

I thanked him for telling me and that I needed to think about it. But I knew it was a good idea. My life was ending and I kept telling myself that I needed to spend more time with friends. This was the time. I didn't need to wait any longer. A week later I moved in with Frank but despite the new situation and the welcome distraction of his company I kept thinking about Vicky.

One day while Frank was at work I drove to St.

Louis. I had talked to Vicky a few days earlier and knew she didn't have class or work. My stomach tumbled as I drove. I never thought of turning back. I hoped she was alone. But I didn't know what to do when I saw her. A kiss? A hug? Or just talk. It could be my imagination and maybe it would ruin everything. I tried to tell myself that was fine since I was dying. It didn't work. I didn't want to screw up the relationship. I wanted her to always have fond memories.

As I parked, fears surfaced. If Brent were there he would hate me. Maybe he would hate her. I didn't want that. I didn't want to ruin her relationship. I just wanted to see what our life would be. Just a snapshot. It felt utterly foolish. Selfish. I thought of leaving. Starting my car and driving home. It was a nice enough day. It wouldn't be a complete waste.

But I am a fool. I got out and started walking to their place. I told myself I would just talk to her. Tell her I had driven up here for an appointment. I was so nervous or maybe it was the tumor's effects. And at the bottom of the stairs nausea struck me. I bent over in the grass. Heaved. Vomited on the clean grass. A door shut.

Are you okay?

I didn't look up but recognized her voice.

Dughall?

I looked at her with my sick face.

Hey.

What are you doing here?

I was just in the area. Had an appointment.

I thought you weren't going to any more doctors?

Well you never can be sure I guess.

I'm glad you are. Did you need to come inside and clean up?

I nodded. Stomach still sick. Churning. I followed her. She wore sweatpants and a tight fitting short sleeve top. Her hair was pulled back in a ponytail like women do when they are home alone. There were no words as we ascended the stairs. And none as we entered the apartment. It was empty. Brent was working. But all I wanted now was for her to be a friend.

Forty-Two

Have a seat.

She waved toward the couch. Her motions appeared desperate. Rushed.

Where's Brent?

He's at work. He was supposed to be off early and home by now but . . . well he hasn't called me yet.

I nodded as she brought a washcloth and dabbed my mouth then put it in a bowl on the table. She gave me a cup. Motioned toward the sink in the kitchen. I went over. Rinsed and spit. She handed me a peppermint. I smiled. She always complained about people's breath. I looked up at her. Her hair was up. Eyelashes long. Black. Cheeks freckled. Lips pursed in concentration. We walked over to the couch and sat down. I glanced over at her.

How are you? How's school?

I'm alright. School's okay. I'm ready to be done. You know the whole senior itch thing? How are you? How is . . . everything?

It's okay, just trying to enjoy my time.

Dughall . . . I don't want you to die.

I looked away.

I don't want that either but it happens to everyone. It's just that I know it could be any day now. I can't control it and my life has been one downward spiral after another. Ever since my parents passed away it seems like someone else I'm close to has died each year. I'm sick of it really. I mean, who would be next? Frank? You? I couldn't bear that.

Dughall you're so young. I don't want you to go.

She took my hand. Sandwiching it between hers. She didn't pull away as I kissed her lips. They trembled, massaging mine. One of her hands moved from my hand to my cheek. Her touch so perfectly feminine as she slowly stroked my face. Our mouths opened and I felt her tongue in mine. She pulled away, hand still on my cheek.

I can't do this Dughall. I can't screw up my relationship with Brent.

I know. I'm sorry. I really am. I had to see what it would be like between you and me. I had to. I'm so sorry.

She sat there a moment. Silent. Absorbing the situation. I inched away. Uncomfortable. Waiting for her to tell me to go. Never come back. She laughed. She bent over on the couch and laughed. She looked at me. Face red. Smiling.

Dughall, did you come all the way here to do that? Did you?

I didn't say anything. My cheeks burned.

You did, didn't you? Oh god, Dughall, why would you wait until now? Of all times? I feel like Brent is never here. And I don't know. I don't know if I love him anymore. And now you. That kiss. And you are . . . you are dying. I just . . .

Her face lowered. Slow sobs made her body convulse. Instinctively I held her. It was something I had done many times before. Holding her after letdowns and breakups and deaths. She stuck her face into my chest. Her sobs subsided. I felt her kiss my neck. My lips caressed hers. She raised her head. Eyes even with mine telling me she wanted me. Telling me she wished things were different. And I kissed her lips.

Forty-Three

We scrambled as footsteps echoed on the stairs. She pulled away, jumping to the other side of the couch. I froze. Waiting to hear the key click. The footsteps stopped and I stood up, a nervous smile on my face.

I'm going to the bathroom.

She smiled, nodded and slapped my ass as I rose.

I went in the bathroom. Crossed my fingers as I peed. I heard key turn and door open. Washed my hands. I heard them talking.

Hey babe, is that Dughall's car in the parking lot?

Hey honey. Yeah he's in the bathroom.

His voice grew soft and I could no longer make out words. I knew what he was telling her. I opened the door. He turned. Glaring at me. Vicky fidgeted with a cup and looked into it.

Hey Brent. What's up?

I don't want you alone with her, understand?

His face was stern. Almost aggressive. His chest thrust outward. I stared into his eyes. They said everything. They were uncertain, wanted to be tough. I smirked. I had fought next to Dmitri in many fights in high school. I was intimidated by most of the fighters then. But I wasn't afraid now. Maybe I didn't give a damn. Or maybe Brent wasn't a real threat.

Sorry man. I had an appointment nearby and

wanted to stop in.

Vicky put her hand on his bicep. She didn't say anything but he took a deep breath. His chest relaxed.

I don't care. I'm not comfortable with this!

He brushed Vicky's hand off and took a step toward me. I didn't look at Vicky but I saw her glance at me from behind Brent. I should've felt guilty but I didn't. Just awkward. I wanted to leave.

Look, I know Vicky has been wanting to spend time with you so I'll leave you two alone. It was nice talking to you Vicky. And nice to see you, Brent.

He stood like a board. She walked to me and I gave her a hug. It was soft. Distanced. She didn't look at me. I walked to him. Extended my hand. We shook. He held mine tight. Never taking his eyes from mine. He didn't trust me. And he shouldn't. My life now felt reckless. I had nothing to lose. Nothing to gain. I was dying. He knew this. I could devastate this relationship. But I didn't want this. I wanted her to live happily ever after. And she would. She's that type of girl. But I was reckless. I had to try and if Brent knew that, I don't think he would've blamed me.

I thought about a lot on the way home. Cari. Dmitri. Vicky. Brent. But as darkness spread across the highway and the sunset melted into Kansas I thought of Jessica Hall. What had it meant for me to hit her? Why was I chosen to bear this? Was there even any choosing? What was she trying to tell me? Maybe she was telling me to not be afraid. And I was not. But now, it was liberating to know I had this short window. And maybe that was Jessica Hall living through me. Maybe not. I don't know. Maybe my life existed to respect hers. Give her what she never had. I wondered what that could be. And I knew.

Her mother had given me harsh words. She never wanted to hear from me again. I had never seen Jessica's mother but I knew she must be set in her ways. As everyone is. But she was harsh. Critical. She must've been hard on Jessica. Probably nothing she ever did was good enough. And maybe Jessica wanted to befriend me instead of striking me with fear.

Forty-Four

When I walked in, Frank was sitting in the living room. He looked like a lonely old man. Diminutive glasses on his face. Body cross-legged and pensively rocking as he read a book. I smiled as I imagined him with a pipe in his mouth fifty years older. Neither of us said anything. I descended downstairs and was struck by loneliness. A soft breath spread throughout my body realizing that this was my chance to reach out to Frank. Maybe he was lonely. Maybe this wasn't a projection of myself onto him. Slowly I walked back upstairs. I felt a strange dejection as if somehow I needed to apologize to Frank for my own thoughts. I walked to the fridge pulling out a beer.

Wanna a beer Frank?

There was a calm silence as I imagined him cautiously reading the remainder of his prose. Tenderly inserted bookmark. Closed book and removed his glasses.

Sure.

Opening the beer I handed it to him. He smiled.

What's up?

Just doing a lot of thinking right now.

We both took a sip of beer and I felt like I was sitting on the back of Dmitri's truck sharing a warm silent moment like the old days.

You know, I think I've been trying to reconcile everything that happened. I guess that's natural . . . but my accident, losing Dmitri and Cari, it all happened so close together. And my tumor. Vicky. It's like god or whatever is testing me. Trying my patience, my soul. Driving me to either fail or succeed. Even that backpacking trip was a test. I've been asking why this is happening and focusing so much on the search for this answer that the present has become a dream. I've taken so much for granted, Vicky and you. I've just been so selfish.

You don't need to apologize Dughall. We all have tough times and when friends help us out it's hard to focus on good deeds. We're often so immersed in our own shit that we forget about everything outside ourselves. And your situation, I'm sure, has cast doubt and maybe even guilt onto you. Jung said that terrible things often become easily forgetful and we return quickly to 'normalcy' but that we also force guilt upon ourselves.

Yeah I guess maybe I've felt guilty for it all. Maybe I could've stopped the car sooner or swerved more to avoid Jessica. Maybe I should've stayed with Cari and Dmitri. Maybe I should've been there more for Cari. Maybe I should've been more loving. Maybe I'm the reason everything happened. Maybe it's all me . . . all these thoughts constantly flood my mind making me wonder what I could've done. But in the back of my head I feel like it was all meant to be somehow. Maybe it's to help me grow. I don't really know, it's all still a mystery.

He took a swig like Dmitri used to do.

You know sometimes I wish we were back in high school. Remember all those moments when we just didn't care. Burnouts in the school parking lot, smoking cigarettes, drinking cheap whiskey between class. Those were my favorite years I think. Now . . . now it seems like it's all so complicated.

He waved at his massive bookshelf.

I look to these books for guidance and understanding. They certainly give me more than my parents ever could. But I don't understand why I keep losing people. Dmitri and Cari and now you are dying, you know? Vicky has moved away. It's just kind of fucked up. I'm not going to have anyone from the old days when you're gone.

He took a gulp of beer and stared at his cigarette. His immediate silence triggered within me a sadness, an understanding that everything we were taught by our parents and teachers wasn't enough. It wasn't the right knowledge. I felt for him. I felt bad about my self-pity.

That's true Frank. None of what I was told growing up prepared me for death or loss of love but I guess that's really how life is supposed to be, you know? We gotta learn for ourselves what to do, where to turn. It sucks. I wish I wasn't dying. That I wasn't leaving you. It's certainly not my choice. But hang in there for me will you? Live a long life. I can't, you know?

He nodded.

Nostalgia and relief wafted through my body. An emotional connection, the one I had shared so often with Dmitri reemerged. I was glad I had come upstairs and had this beer with Frank.

My vision problems increased over the next few days. Sometimes it was only blurry. But increasingly I saw everything in doubles. I had a hard time driving and had to ask Frank to drive me to Dr. Masterson's office. Dr. Masterson looked happy to see me. His eyes brightened when he walked in.

Dughall, good to see you. You look well.

Thanks you.

You are experiencing diplopia?

I shrugged.

Double vision. I'm quite surprised that you are just now having these issues. It usually happens earlier. How are your headaches and nausea? Are you still taking your Temozolomide?

Headaches seem like they are always there but their severity depends day to day. Nausea is about the same. And yeah still taking the Temo. Is there anything we can do about these vision problems?

Well, really there isn't much we can do unless you decide to follow through with my recommendations of chemotherapy. I would suggest maybe wearing an eye patch. That might help. But really Dughall, I wish you would go for additional treatment. Chemo will most likely prolong your life.

I shook my head.

I'm okay with my decision.

Dr. Masterson was silent. His face looked at the floor then back up at me. He rose and as many men had before, patted my shoulder. Told me to call if I needed anything. I nodded. I walked outside to wait for Frank. The days were shorter now. A quick hard rain had fallen while I had been inside. The pavement was black. Slick. The air heavy with humidty. I faced south, thinking of the wilderness that had been my home for a few days. The purple pink sky flushed with yellow rays. Birds swallowing bugs. Coyotes howling. Bears foraging. I wondered if it were snowing there.

I lit a cigarette. Still looking toward the Ozark mountains, I thought of Vicky. We hadn't talked since our kiss. I took out my cellphone and called her.

Dughall?! How are you?

Hey Vicky. Doing pretty good. Just wondered how you were.

Good. I miss you. I never thought I would be that girl you know? I want see you. You should have someone there with you.

I have Frank.

I know, but I could help you more. I'm more motherly than he is. I want to be with you now Dughall. I want to hold you and talk with you.

I don't think that's a good idea. Brent is a good guy. He loves you. I can never give you that. I do love you but not the same way he does. I will only tear you apart leaving you no one. Brent will move on. He will be resentful. More of me than you, but he probably wouldn't take you back. He's that type of man. He already doesn't like me. Don't hurt him anymore than I already have.

She was silent. The parking lot was silent too. I took a drag on my cigarette and thought of the crisp cold snow on the hills. How it would crunch under my feet. How it would crackle as it feel off the trees.

I won't.

What?

I won't hurt him. I already told him about us. Our kisses. He said he already knew.

A rigid shiver shuddered through my torso. Her heart will be broken. And his. All because of me.

We can't. Vicky. We can't.

I closed my phone as Frank pulled up. I don't know if he said hello. I don't remember buckling my seatbelt or the ride home. Frank asked what was up. I barely heard him. And as we drove, I saw her. For the first time in a while she stood in the road. Frank did not slow down. I did not flinch as we passed through her. I wanted to join her.

Forty-Five

Frank lit a cigarette.

Hey you know I'm going up to St. Louis this weekend. You wanna come? We could swing by and see Vicky and Brent.

I'm not sure.

I talked to Vicky on the phone the other day. She said they are doing better. Brent said he wants to make it work. He loves her. Doesn't want to lose her.

I nodded.

I guess if you'll be there it'll be alright. So yeah, it'd be good to see her. And him.

We sat in silence as I had imagined we would when we were old men in a nursing home. Cigarette smoke curling above our heads imitating our thoughts. The smell of coffee and cigarettes wafted under our noses as we waited for the next topic. It could be anything. There was no limit for two men who had no need for conventional conversation. I looked over at the bookshelf, reading titles and names recognizing that most of them were dead.

Where do you think we go? I said.

What? You mean when we die? I think there's an emptiness, nothingness, we are just gone. Like an unconsciousness. Or maybe there is some sort of afterlife though I doubt any of the theories are correct.

Yeah it's like sin. A scare tactic. And it must not be that scary to the people preaching it or those claiming to hold it as their truth judging by all the greed, lust, sex and sodomy in the churches today. If they truly believed that shit could send you to hell they wouldn't do it.

True. They also have their forgiveness which psychologically gets them out of anything.

Psychological affirmation.

Exactly. But your question, if there is some sort of afterlife, no one can speculate what happens. There have been a lot of people who say they've had visions of heaven or whatever you want to call it but no one will ever know until they've experienced it. It will always be a mystery. I personally am just living the way I want.

I nodded. Lingering on his mention of visions. Frank took a sip of beer.

There's only one life that I know of so I live it how I'm comfortable. Dmitri, he lived his life in a different way. I never identified with him but I think he would be satisfied with most of what he did. If we could talk to him today I don't think he would have many regrets. I think that's maybe what people should focus on instead of where they're going. Their mentality just makes them live in fear of the inevitable. I think in a lot of ways I follow their commandments more than they do.

I thought about my life. Not the death or depression or anxieties but the times in between which were more prevalent. The times with Dmitri when we would go mudding in places we weren't supposed to. Street racing with the sound of sirens in the distance. Making love in the back of hot rods. Drinking. Smoking. Sharing conversations with Dmitri, Frank, Cari and others that sometimes were humorous stories others somber or intellectual discussions. It all made sense. I smiled and nodded at Frank, smoked my cigarette and took out Dmitri's flask.

Fuck.

Forty-Six

Frank insisted on driving to St. Louis. My vision problems were worse now. We pulled into the small apartment parking lot. I saw Vicky running out of her building, down the stairs as we got out.

Dughall!

I was glad Brent was with her. And Frank with me. I was tempted to continue our kiss.

Hey, Vicky. I've missed you.

She held a finger up.

Don't say that.

Sorry. It's good to see you.

I extended my hand to Brent and as we shook, he covered our hands with his other hand, face grimacing.

I'm sorry we've had our differences Dughall.

I nodded.

I'm sorry too. I'm really sorry.

Vicky squeezed his arm. I smiled.

Dughall, I . . . we've got something to show you. Come on inside.

She bounced up to their apartment full of energy like always. I was happy she would never change. Walking into the apartment I took a deep breath it smelled like a pumpkin candle, one of my favorite smells. Vicky walked to her dresser and handed me a piece of paper. My heart skipped bringing a nervousness I hadn't felt much since I knew I would die.

It was a bill of sale with my handwriting.

Vehicle Sold: 1970 Chevrolet Nova

Owner: Dughall Martin

Sold to: Steve Garard

Next to his name was a phone number in Frank's handwriting, a date and an address in Vicky's handwriting. The date was today. Her smile reminded me of the last day of high school and the time I took her on a drag race for the first time and when she used to talk about Brent. I said nothing as I stared at the paper. I had dreamed of seeing the Nova again, often wishing I hadn't sold it.

I slapped Frank on the shoulder and chuckled.

You've been going through my shit, you bastard!

He smiled.

Vicky giggled. Hugging me.

We meet up with him in an hour outside of Wentzville. Let's go! she said.

Jumping into the car with my three friends my heartbeat quickened, realizing I would see the car I had never stopped loving. Its memory like any youthful remembrance had grown larger than life and though tainted with an unpleasant memory I still loved her. I rubbed my hands together and lived vicariously through Vicky's vocal excitement. Brent drove as Frank and I stared out our respective windows. Every so often we hummed a chorus to a song on the radio or injected our opinions into Vicky's commentary.

Steve's house was a well-kept white ranch off a country road. It looked immaculate. As we got out one of the garage doors opened revealing Steve and behind him, I saw it. Now baby blue, she held the same expression she had for the five years I had her. She looked happy. I took a deep breath as Vicky squealed and clapped her hands. Frank squeezed my shoulder.

Hey Dughall, it's been a while.

Steve walked up to me grasping my hand like an old friend.

Hi Steve. How are you?

Good.

He turned to Vicky and Brent.

You must be Vicky. And you are Frank?

I'm Brent, Vicky's boyfriend. That's Frank.

Frank lifted his hand.

Good to meet you all.

He motioned me to the Nova. Frank started to follow but Vicky held him back. I shot her a curious stare. She smiled. I followed Steve as he talked about what he had done to the car, paint and interior in particular but to my surprise the drive train remained intact.

It ran so good I had to leave it that way, he said.

I walked around the car and noticed him stop by

the driver's door looking at the concrete floor.

Dughall . . . Vicky told me you have a terminal brain tumor.

I nodded.

My father and brother passed away from cancer. I'm truly sorry.

Unsure what to say what kind of response he needed from me, I continued looking at the car trying not to let it get to me.

I want you to drive it.

I stopped, looked at the clean blue body lines that used to be rough gray primer.

I can't . . .

Yeah Dughall, I've thought about it. You deserve to have one more ride. We're the same, you and me. We love this car. She demands respect. I insist.

I've been having vision problems.

I tried to make an excuse, afraid that I would screw up this beautiful car.

Holding out the keys he smiled.

I don't care. Take her for a spin. Show me how you used to drive her.

Forty-Seven

I got in, trying to suppress my excitement and worry. Vicky jumped up and down, clapping as I bumped the key. It turned like it always had. Belching. Engine that fast drumbeat. Bumpity bipppity bumpity. Up on the trigger under the hammerhead knob shifter pulling it back from park to drive. Engine dropping tempo. Bumpity bipppity bumpity. I pulled out of the garage into the sunlit perfect fall day.

I returned Frank's grin as I eased out of the driveway, Steve silent next to me. The car idled up to the end of the drive and I looked out onto the country road.

Give it hell Dughall.

I glanced over at him to acknowledge his direction. He nodded and smiled. I waited for a car to go by and pulled out. Slow at first so the back of the car wouldn't swing out too much. Then I hammered the gas. The engine roared. My hands gripped the wheel and the back swung sideways. The spinning tires carried it back and forth leaving behind a trail of thick white smoke and curvy black lines. Tachometer light glowed blue as I slammed the shifter forward into second gear. I felt it all. Gasoline igniting pistons pumping crankshaft spinning pushing power through torque converter into transmission to the back wheels.

I felt at one with the car. My foot to the floor as

the transmission shifted to the third and final gear. Steve held tight to the door and I pushed the car as I had in every race, fearing nothing but losing. I glanced down at the speedometer as it spun past 120 mph. I slowed, letting off the gas, dragging the car down to below 100. I hit the brakes softly to maintain a speed close to the limit. The engine hummed, methodically massaging my body. In memory of Dmitri I slammed on the brakes, turning wheel rapidly to cause a controlled spin the car spun around facing the other direction. Still sliding I pushed on the gas and the back of car fishtailing wickedly left and right before straightening and headed back to Steve's house. He did not speak for a few seconds.

I've never driven this car like that . . .

I said nothing, thinking only of Dmitri. Arriving back at Steve's I felt a calm excitement when he invited us inside for dinner. His children were young. Five and seven but seemed much older. His wife was a kind, quiet woman who reminded me of a grandmother constantly offering us drinks and food, yearning to take care of us in that Midwestern way. Over dinner we talked of Dmitri. The old days. Hanging out in the Nova. Steve seemed to enjoy it, no doubt filing these stories away to add to the Nova's history. Before leaving Steve asked why I had sold the Nova. I told him the story that seemed so distant now. So lost. As I got in Vicky's car Steve grabbed my shoulder, pulling me back to give me a large hug.

Forty-Eight

The car was silent but for a blistering guitar solo blared from the speakers. It seemed appropriate. Vicky appeared exhausted but content. Brent's face concentrated on the road. Frank peered out his window. I looked around admiring the colors of the sunset. It spread yellow, pink, purple, red across the spacious Missouri sky. I dug in my pocket and pulled out Cari's poem and read it. I glanced up as we passed a sign for a nature area at the next exit, I caressed the paper before tucking it back in my pocket and said, Can we stop at that nature area?

Brent looked over at Vicky, whose face said she didn't feel like it.

Um . . . sure Dughall. We can stop.

I nodded as we left the highway. We drove up a gravel road to a parking lot. I could smell the Missouri River and feel the cool air as it brushed my nose. I didn't wait to see if anyone else would get out. Instead I started walking briskly.

Dughall?

Vicky yelled behind me, a worried slightly irritated tone. I turned motioning her to follow me. I didn't slow down but walked toward the trees that buffered my view of the river. The sunset waning now, giving everything a yellow Midwest hue. Fallen leaves lined the tree-line, grass forfeiting their green space. The silent whoosh of the magnificent river nearby whispered. Looking up, I marveled at the tall trees, their branches dropping leaves. Acorns spread like gracious fingers dripping with honey.

I walked through the trees, sending tiny shockwaves up my feet as leaves, branches and acorns crunched. The sun shone behind me as I headed east through the foliage, its life barely visible now as dusk began its slow descent. I hear Vicky yelling behind me. I keep going, I wanted to see the river.

I arrived at a ripe green grass clearing overlooking the river and felt at ease. As I sat there a hawk screeched and an owl queried. The breeze was cool but I barely noticed, my eyes fixed in the fading light on the river rushing in front of me, forever moving forward to the ocean. It seemed so far away. I thought about Cari and how we had been at the ocean. I thought of her face and how it glowed in the sunset. I wished she was here.

Vicky's voice grew closer. I felt her footsteps vibrating on the ground. My body collapsed on the cool grass. The trees clustered above me, circling in dark shadowy figures. Dmitri's flask shifted its weight in the chest pocket of my coat. It pressed against my chest. My eyes closed. I could smell Vicky. A hair tickled my nose. Everything faded.

I opened them to look down at my shoeless feet and rose and walked through a cool creek on my grandfather's farm. Everyone was there. My grandparents,

parents, Dmitri and Cari. My mother and grandmothers chatted on the shore. My paternal grandfather skipped rocks next to me. My maternal grandfather came and held my hand as we walked. He was silent. Looking forward. Slight smile. My father walked on the bank beside us. Dmitri walked behind us. Telling stories. Cari strode over grabbing my other hand. I looked at her. Her face glowed. And smiled.

From the banks of the shallow creek birds sang. Deer nodded. Squirrels chattered. The trees seemed greener than normal. Soft leaves brushed our faces from low hanging limbs. We walked for what seemed hours. Arriving downstream we looked over a cliff. The water cascaded over a rock face. The sun was setting. Its colors so vibrant everything looked like it was on fire. I felt like I could reach out and touch it.

We walked off the cliff. I hesitated. Expecting fear, anxiety. There was none. I was at ease. I floated as we descended like an elevator then walked back up even with the cliff. Our speed increased rapidly like a plane on a runway. Nothing but comfort compelled me as we careened toward a figure. I recognized it as Jessica Hall. She stood. Hands outstretched as in the accident. Her face contorted and frightened. We stopped inches from her and hovered.

In the memory that has haunted me she stared at me. Eyes wide and fearful. At first I was afraid. But everything stopped. It froze. Trees rose around us as we descended back into the creek. My grandmothers talked, Dmitri told stories. My grandfather and Cari held my hands. Jessica still stood. Arms outstretched as the sun faded revealing the largest most brilliant moon surrounded by a million perfect stars.

I let go of my grandfather and Cari's hands walking to Jessica, this time with my arms outstretched. All conversation stopped and I felt each eye upon us. We advanced. As we neared each other I saw a large thankful smile upon her face. As we embraced everything went calm and black.

ACKNOWLEDGMENTS

Much love and thanks to my wife for her support and my cats for their entertainment throughout the writing of this novel.

I'm deeply grateful to my parents, my sisters, Ben Cassil, Mandy Cassil, Frank Streng, Alice Streng, Lottie Ingalls and Brenda Pope.

And finally, a special thanks goes out to everyone in The People's Ink, especially; Richard Pope, Dave Garlock, Kai Soderberg, C.I. DeMann, Jason Arquin, Anise Leinen, Tom Turner, Jim O'Neal, Paul McKlendin, Adam Stonewall, Hillary Woolley, Krista Humphrey, Charles Finks, Robert Benefiel and all of my friends who have shown their kindness and support throughout the years.

www.ingramcontent.com/pod-product-compliance
Lightning Source LLC
Chambersburg PA
CBHW030324180626
46810CB00003B/1219